MURDER
BY
DEATH

A Novel by
HENRY KEATING

Based on the Original
Screenplay by
NEIL SIMON

WARNER BOOKS

A Warner Communications Company

WARNER BOOKS EDITION
First Printing: May, 1976
Second Printing: July, 1976

Warner Books, Inc., 75 Rockefeller Plaza, New York, N.Y. 10019

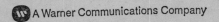 A Warner Communications Company

Printed in the United States of America

Not associated with Warner Press, Inc. of Anderson, Indiana

1

"No!"

The voice rang in rage round the high, book-lined walls of the library in the old house.

"No, no, no, no, no. It can't be. It mustn't be. It's too bad. It's too damn bad."

Lionel Twain, eighteenth richest man in the world —no, sorry, seventeenth: reports have just come in of the unfortunate decease of the current No. 17, who had triplet heirs—the *seventeenth* richest man in the world, flung the book he had just finished all the way from one end of his library to the other.

And that was quite a throw. The place was anything up to thirty yards long, and every yard of its walls was lined with books. Books in fine old musty calf bindings. Books with elegant gold-tooled lettering on their spines. Books as beautiful as books could be made to be. And each last one of them a murder mystery. Including the one Lionel Twain had just hurled with such violence along the whole length of the room.

He sat up straighter in his big leather-covered armchair and glared at the huge, inoffensive fire in the huge, inoffensive fireplace.

"No," he repeated, his voice still choked with fury. "It just isn't good enough. The millionth mystery I've read, and a damned silly, unlikely solution, just like all the other nine hundred and ninety-nine thousand, nine hundred and ninety-nine. *No. No. No!* This just *cannot* go on."

He rang the bell by his side for Benson, his faithful butler. A drink was all that was in his mind at that moment. A large and very powerful drink. The sort of drink that could take the mind of the seventeenth richest man in the world off his troubles, even off the terrible discovery that having read, in pursuit of his pet hobby, no fewer than one million mystery stories, each and every one of them had a damned unsatisfactory, altogether too-brilliant-to-be-possible ending.

But by the time Benson had arrived—and he had a long, long way to come from the kitchen quarters of this big, old, isolated house—Lionel Twain had an altogether different request to make. And there was on his face an altogether different expression.

Gone was his glare of baffled fury. In its place was a look of grim determination. And when a man like Twain, who became rich by his own efforts (or up until that last promotion, anyway) gets determined, then anyone or anything in his way had better get out fast or agree to do just what he, she, or it is told. A little dynamo was Lionel Twain, a little atom-powered dynamo.

"Benson!" he roared (his roar sounded a bit like a mouse's, but let that pass). "Benson, bring me some deckle-edged invitation cards. Goddammit, bring me five deckle-edged invitation cards."

In the twinkling of an eye five invitation cards, thick, pure white, and very, very deckle-edged, were lying on a silver salver in front of him. (Lucky old Benson had remembered a pack of invitation cards in a drawer of Twain's big, dark oak desk, and they had been deckle-edged down to the last one).

"Benson," said Lionel Twain, "here's what I'm going to do."

"Yes, sir."

"Oh, by the way, first would you pick up that calf-bound volume you see down at the far end of the room. It's lying on the floor. I can't think how it got there."

"No, sir, most mysterious," Benson said, setting off on the long walk.

"Most mysterious, most mysterious. Damn good, it's a mystery. Most mysterious. Damn good."

Lionel Twain was easily amused. When *he* made the jokes.

He had hardly finished giggling when Benson got back with the millionth discarded mystery.

"Now, listen, Benson," his master said, wiping his eyes. "We're going to give a dinner party."

"Indeed, sir."

Benson was an English-trained butler and knew all about murmuring a discreet "Indeed, sir" at regular intervals.

"Yes, indeed, Benson. And guess who we are going to invite."

"Whom are we going to invite, sir?"

Benson was pretty good, too, at discreetly correcting any appalling ignorance on the subject of grammar that might fall from his transatlantic master's lips. They cannot help it, he would often think to himself charitably, they just have not been born with the right advantage. I mean, having to live under a President . . . Well, you could hardly expect *grammar* in the circumstances.

"Benson," replied Lionel Twain, unabashed at this discreet correction, because you don't get to be as rich as he if you listen to anybody attempting to tell you anything. "Benson, we're going to invite the five greatest detectives in all written history to dinner. And, Benson . . ."

"Yes, sir."

Very discreet, very Benson.

"Benson, we're going to provide them with a murder mystery that's going to show them they're not one half so damned clever as they think themselves."

"Indeed, sir."

Lionel Twain would have liked a bit of a stronger reaction to his wonder plan. But he knew that he didn't employ an English-trained butler for nothing. Service you got. Discreet murmurs you got. Grammatical corrections you got. But awed surprise you had to do without.

Or supply yourself.

"Yes, Benson, you are going to witness the greatest mystery of all time. And you're going to see with your own eyes today's five greatest sleuths ending up totally and completely baffled."

"Indeed, sir?" murmured Benson.

But was there in that discreet murmur a hint, just a hint, of disbelief? Had Benson, in his secret soul, down there beneath the starch, a little burning faith in the great detectives whose exploits he too had read in those million calf-bound volumes that ranged the walls of the big old library? Was Benson saying to himself "We'll see"?

He was.

Yet in due course five invitations went out from the old house in remote Lola Lane. Five invitations printed in black on large white cards deckle-edged with gold. And Lionel Twain was certain that though some of his guests lived half across the globe from this shadow-filled and rain-lashed Victorian house looking down on the great city of San Francisco, each of them would come within the time he had set. The terms of his invitation made sure of that. It read:

You are cordially invited to dinner . . .
and a MURDER

Then followed the details.

The place: *22 Lola Lane, San Francisco*. The day: *On Saturday next*. The time: *At 7 p.m.*

From a pile of envelopes on the old oak desk in the library Lionel Twain's small white hands reached for the top one which lay face downward in the strong pool of light which fell from a tall, heavy desk lamp. They plucked it up. For a moment they held it delicately by its edges, a thick white envelope, ready for a thick white deckle-edged invitation card. Then, with a sudden twist, they turned it over.

The envelope was already addressed, a hand-written address in thick black flourish-filled writing. The writing of the signature, Lionel Twain. A curious hand. An expert graphologist might make a meal of its

8

loops and swirls, its flourishes and its curlicues. Except that Lionel Twain took good care that very few specimens of his handwriting were available for expert examination under the microscope of forensic graphologists. He was a very careful man, Lionel Twain.

That would show up in any analysis of the way he formed his words. Extreme carefulness. A talent, a genius, for not making careless slips. That and a talent, a genius even, for the macabre, the flourish of grim showmanship that makes sure that every twist and turn of the mind tells to its full potential.

In fact, the knowledge of that will draw these very distinguished guests to the dinner table. It will draw, surely as a giant electromagnet reaching into the dark night, the first guest whose name is on the thick white envelope which Lionel Twain has just flicked into view.

Mr. Dick Charleston . . . with Mrs. Dora Charleston and Pet Terrier

Dick Charleston, one of the half-dozen most world-famed detectives. Dick Charleston, smooth and sophisticated as an ice-fired martini, once the ace operator for the Pan-American Investigation Agency, since retired and happily married to the sweetest, sharpest, wise-crackingest heiress from Cape Cod to the Golden Gate, his dearest companion save a certain Myron, inseparable, face-licking Myron . . .

The first card slid smoothly into its thick envelope. The envelope was lifted, passed out of the cone of light from the ornate lamp, made brief contact in the shadow beyond with a tongue, a little, pointed, very pink tongue, and was firmly sealed.

In the light Lionel Twain reached for the next envelope. Again he held it carefully for a few long seconds between the tips of his elegantly manicured fingers while the name, still hidden face-down on the surface of the richly dark oak desk, was pondered, mulled over, savored.

Then, flick.

And the bright light revealed it, to Twain's apparent delight.

9

Inspector Sidney Wang,
care of Police Headquarters, Cataline, Calif.

Little doubt that Sidney Wang, the Hawaiian-Chinese detective every bit as celebrated as Dick Charleston, the enigmatic clue-solver extraordinary, will accept this mystery invitation for next Saturday, to dinner and a murder, a murder premeditated to this degree!

A peal of thunder obliterated what might have been a chuckle emanating from the darkness of the big library just beyond the falling light from the lamp. Or perhaps it was only the fire settling in the big chimney-place . . .

And the third card was picked up, held suspensefully between the tips of well-manicured fingers and twisted to the light.

Monsieur Milo Perrier,
Blackharbour Mansions, London W.1, England

Milo Perrier, cocky little Belgian sleuth, for long established in the England to which he had come as a refugee in the early days of World War One, master of the little gray cells, proud possessor of *moustaches formidables,* will be totally unable to refuse it. To be present when a murder is *committed.* Why, it will surely only be a matter of the swift exercise of the processes deductive and the murderer will be unmasked. Yes, no doubt, *Monsieur* Milo Perrier will come hurrying across the Atlantic (much though he detests travel) to take dinner here at No. 22 Lola Lane next Saturday evening. And, be sure, if the invitation says 7 p.m., promptly at 7 p.m. he will arrive.

A flick of the wicked pink tongue. Letter No. 3 was sealed, and once more Lionel Twain held another envelope face down, keeping the pleasure of contemplating the name already written there till the last moment.

A vivid flash of lightning seared across the tall windows of the high old room. It flickered green and purple. And before the following crack of thunder came, the envelope was switched round. The name written blackly upon it was plain to see.

Mr. Sam Diamond

Sam Diamond, the name. And the address? A beat-up office in downtown San Francisco. An office with a battered swivel chair behind an equally battered desk, a brass ashtray on it always half-filled with butts, gray flakes of ash forever dotting the papers scattered on it. An office with a buff-curtained window, open just sometimes when there happens to be no fog to counter the oppressive heat. From the narrow court outside comes a slow current of air faintly scented with ammonia, enough just to cause the ashes on the desk to twitch and crawl before falling back onto some other patch of the green blotter. A private eye's office. In the battered filing cabinet behind the desk, a bottle of bourbon and half a dozen waiting paper cups.

But what a private eye. The one *everybody* knows. The one who never just solves a case, he busts it. Busts it wide open.

Sam Diamond was not exactly a tuxedo-wearing regular dinner guest. But Sam Diamond would most certainly accept an invitation to dinner next Saturday night.

Flick, flick went the little pink tongue. A little cough came from the shadows beyond the cone of lamplight. A little self-satisfied cough. Or was that the logs on the fire crumbling again into their red bed?

One more. For the last time an envelope was reached for, held in suspense, and flicked to the light.

Miss Jessica Marbles,
Church Cottage, Mead St. Mary, Sussex, England

What was an address like that doing in this pile of envelopes? Could the possessor of the handwriting that showed such extreme carefulness have made a slip? Already?

No, Miss Jessica Marbles may be no professional detective. She is as far from being a policeman or even a policewoman as a tabby cat is from a tiger. But in her time she has solved mysteries with the best of them. There was the occasion when the famed movie star went to the gallows in dear old England because he shared certain character traits with a grocer's boy who had jilted his sweetheart. There was

11

the matter of the millionaire who seemed such a philanthropist but whose face so strongly reminded Miss Marbles of the face of the village Scoutmaster who once made off with all twenty-eight pounds, three shillings and fourpence in the seaside outing fund. And that millionaire was prevented just in time from leaving dear old England's shores with a million pounds' worth of bearer bonds stuffed in the bottom of his crocodile-skin suitcase.

No, when it came to crime, Miss Marbles could hold her own. And, though an elderly lady might find it difficult to travel the Atlantic and across the whole stretch of the mighty United States, there could be no doubt that, come next Saturday, Jessica Marbles would be sitting down to dine at No. 22 Lola Lane, San Francisco—fog or no fog. Miss Jessica Marbles was a damned determined old lady.

The last of the letters met the kiss of the little pink tongue. Sealed, it rested on the pile with the others. An over-white hand stretched across the dark surface of the magnificent desk and rang a small brass bell.

The sound tinkled out into the darkness of the great old house and died away. Silence resumed its sway. Distantly, the thunder rumbled once or twice and the rain beat steadily against the tall windows.

Then through the quiet came a sudden sharp little sound. *Tap.*

Silence again. The rain softly striking against the glass of the tall windows. The fire unmoving now. The figure at the huge desk still as a statue, a waiting statue.

Tap. Tap, tap. Tap, tap, tap. Tap.

Getting moment by moment nearer and nearer, the same little sharp sound in the perfect quiet of the big rambling Victorian house. A sharp little sound, difficult to place.

Outside the lightning, seemingly more distant now, flickered briefly. A pale purple light, greenish-tinged, played over the fat leather armchairs, over the rows and rows of old musty-smelling volumes on the shelves.

Tap, tap. Tap. Tap.

Louder and louder. Nearer and nearer. Irregular.

Clearly to be heard for all that it was faint. Faint as a ghost's footsteps. Tap. Tap, tap, tap. Tap.

Still the figure at the desk did not move. Still the fire in the heavy chimneyplace smoldered. Still the light fell in a clear pool on the five waiting envelopes on the dark surface of the great desk.

Tap, tap, tap. Tap, tap, tap.

Very near now. Right outside the door.

Then silence. Silence inside the book-lined library. Silence outside.

Then, very faintly, hardly to be heard even by the most acute ears, a slithering. A slithering on the far surface of the tall mahogany desk. A soft searching.

The figure at the desk, sitting silently brooding on those five invitations, did not move by so much as a millimeter.

Then the slithering ceased. The searching stopped. Slowly the doorknob turned . . .

"You rang, sir?"

It was Benson. He still looked the very essence of butler, variety slim-line, the deferential expression, the black jacket and the striped trousers, the spirit of quiet tailor-made service, the insinuation that your wants are better known to him than they can possibly be to you.

But there was one thing different about him now. He no longer carried a silver salver on which was placed the exact drink his master did not know he wanted. Instead, loosely held in his right hand was a long light white-painted cane. It was this that had tap-tapped its way from distant servants' quarters to the library. Tapping along the gloomy corridors, tapping up a flight of stairs here, down a flight there, tap-tapping in answer to the summons of the little brass bell. For Benson was bat-blind. On his smooth inquiring face was a pair of dark glasses.

"You rang, sir?"

"Yes," said Twain, "the invitations are ready. Stamp them, will you, and put them in the post. They should go tonight."

"Yes, sir."

From a little box that formed the centerpiece of

13

the desk's brass pen set Twain extracted a handful of postage stamps and thrust them toward Benson.

"Here you are."

Benson took them as if he could see where they were held and placed one to his mouth, licked it, stooped and pressed it home. One by one he dealt with each of the letters, and straightened up.

There spread across the surface of the big desk were the five startlingly white letters. Beside them, firmly adhering to the wood, were five colored stamps.

"You really think they'll come, sir?" Benson inquired with just the merest touch of well-concealed disloyalty.

Sighing a little and scrabbling at the still wet stamps, the master of the house replied with confidence.

"Oh, yes, they'll come, all right. They'll come."

2

Fog everywhere. Fog down in San Francisco Bay where it flowed past Goat Island and Angel Island and Alcatraz. Fog in the streets where it rolled defiled among the blocks of high-rises and the curbside pollutions of a great (and dirty) city. Fog in Chinatown, fog on Nob Hill. Fog creeping into the cabins of the cable cars fog lying up on the roofs and hovering in the TV aerials of tall buildings; fog drooping on the signboards of restaurants and nightclubs. Fog in the eyes and throats of ancient waterfront hookers, wheezing by the screens of their TV sets; fog in the stem and bowl of the evening pipe of the dreamy addict, down in his close cellar; fog cruelly pinching the toes and fingers of his shivering little girl friend on her way to the liquor store. Chance people on Golden Gate Bridge peered from their cars into a sky of fog underneath them, with fog all around them, as if they were in a helicopter and hovering in the mist clouds.

The raw evening was at its rawest, though, and the dense fog was at its densest near those high old Victorian piles that dot either side of Lola Lane out in the remote countryside. And No. 22 Lola Lane was at the very heart of the fog.

Not surprising, since Lionel Twain, master showman of the macabre, had installed in his extensive grounds the biggest goddam fog machine money could buy.

Somewhere out there five cars were creeping their way toward Lola Lane. Five very distinguished people

15

were on their way to a murder. The nearest car was an early Rolls-Royce convertible. A dashing machine this, if not exactly adapted to the present weather. It spoke of chic and sophistication and a fat bank account. It spoke, too, of effortless motoring, of craftsmen-guaranteed reliability. At that precise moment, however, it had stalled.

Dick Charleston, debonair in a latest-fashion dinner suit (rolled lapels) was standing in the roadway looking down at the engine and holding in his right hand, with that inimitable air of expertise that comes from long, long practice, a martini glass. Inside the car sat his wife, Dora, working away mercilessly with compact and powder puff. She wore a dress that would stop anyone thinking about rolled lapels, or any other sort of lapels. It was simply wow, and also very expensive. Definitely not the best kind of protective clothing to be wearing on a damned foggy night. Myron was wiser. Sitting next to Dora he sank into his very own thick woolly coat.

Pretty well adapted, too, was the Rolls itself. Adapted by none other than Lionel Twain.

At considerable expense certain gentlemen in his indirect employ had visited the Charleston garages (yes, enough for five cars) and had equipped the Rolls which Dick always took when they went visiting—it had style, after all—with certain additional optional extras. Like several microphones, an excellent miniature transmitter, and a couple of well-hidden TV cameras.

So every detail of the breakdown was available, in color, on a luxurious screen in a viewing room at No. 22 Lola Lane, San Francisco. And in that viewing room Lionel Twain was observing the proceedings with happy interest.

"Have you found the trouble yet, Dickie?" he heard Dora cooingly inquire.

Where did she get that British accent, for heaven's sake, he wondered. Perhaps the same place as that wow of a dress. They were both equally expensive.

Dick glanced up from the machine-finished intricacies of the Rolls-Royce engine.

"Yes, pet," he answered. "Or anyway, I've narrowed it down."

"Narrowed it down, pet?"

"To the *engine,* pet."

He gave himself a little toast from his martini glass. Could be that he needed it.

"Good work, darling," Dora said loyally.

"Thank you, dear," he replied automatically and distinterestedly.

Dora mulled over the latest information from the front. Myron beside her mulled a bit, too.

Dora arrived at a conclusion.

"Can you fix it, dear?"

"Only if I knew something about engines," Dick replied, baring his inadequacies.

"Mother," Dora remarked, speaking partly to the foggy night without and partly to the doggy friend within, "Mother warned me not to marry a detective."

Myron looked just a little interested but the foggy night did not, and Dora continued, "Mother said, 'Dora, one night you'll find yourself lost on a foggy road on the way to a mysterious house when suddenly your car will go dead and your husband will stand there helplessly looking at the engine and drinking a martini.' "

"Mother said that?" Dick inquired.

"Those very words. She was a bright woman."

"And luckily," Dick added, sotto voce, "very rich."

He gave the intricacies of Mr. Rolls and Mr. Royce another long steady look.

"Ah," he exclaimed. "Would you look in the glove compartment, darling?"

Dora eagerly flipped it open.

"What do you need?" she asked, her voice muffled from having to go into the boxlike compartment before coming out into the foggy night.

"The olives," Dick answered unhesitatingly. "I put the olives in there. Can't really appreciate a martini without an olive."

Dora extracted the olives with wifely obedience.

Myron, the notion of pleasure from tasting having been put into his head, licked Dora's face.

"Myron, please don't lick," she said, as best she could for that rough little pink tongue. "Mommy just powdered."

Conscious that she probably now looked like a richly painted Impressionist picture after an unfortunate encounter with a sandblaster, Dora began to feel a little put out.

"Dickie," she said, "don't you think we'd be better off looking for a telephone?"

Dick was too busy swirling the olive-improved martini over his palate to give her much of a reply.

"In a moment, my pet."

From the darkness came the sudden sound of a howling wolf cry, courtesy of Mr. Lionel Twain and a very costly electronic bullhorn.

"Well," Dick said, unperturbed, "if you're going to whine at me, let's look for your phone."

In the viewing room at No. 22 Lionel Twain watched the three of them set out, Dick carrying his martini bravely before him, Dora hugging her wow of a dress closely around her—not that it was possible for it to be much closer in most places—and Myron trotting along at the end of his leash. Inspired perhaps by Dick's noble example, Twain rang for Benson and a large martini, with olive.

Benson, it turned out, had already guessed that at about this time his master would be requiring a martini —and that the martini would be requiring an olive. He had been standing just behind his master's chair for the past few minutes, watching with calm interest the events taking place in and around the Rolls-Royce convertible.

"It seemed to me, sir," he said smoothly, as he handed the glass on its silver salver, "that Mr. Charleston carried off the discovery of the engine failure with admirable sangfroid."

"Bah," replied Lionel Twain.

"Bah, sir?" Benson inquired.

"Engine failure, bah. I fixed every bit of that. Told my fellows to drain the tank of gas. Silly fool never noticed it. Great Detective, bah."

"Indeed, sir," said Benson.

18

But he said it a little sadly, and inwardly he hoped that before too long Dick Charleston—why, he'd seen every one of the films at least twice—would have a chance of redeeming his reputation.

Meanwhile, out in the fog, our intrepid trio, after a long walk through a countryside ill-equipped with roadside telephones, had at last reached one that seemed to have been placed there just for them.

As, of course, it had. Benson and Twain settled down to watch Part II.

As Dick was thankfully dialing the number for 22 Lola Lane, Lionel Twain reached for a large pair of wire-cutters.

"It's ringing," Dick told Dora, cheerfulness beginning to creep back into his voice.

He looked down at Myron.

"I wonder," he asked Dora, "could you walk him a yard or two away, dear? My leg might appear like a tree in this fog."

In his ear the distant phone rang briskly, expectantly. Before long, help should be on its way.

Dora, standing at a safe distance with Myron, looked around.

"What a godforsaken spot to get lost," she drawled, her cheerfulness not having been kept even at simmering point by frequent applications of alcohol.

"True," Dick agreed, "I saw a much better spot a few miles back."

Dora was *not* amused.

"Haven't they answered that damned phone yet?"

"It's ringing. It'll be a big house they have there. I guess the butler will be making his way steadily along a mile or two of old corridor to get to the phone. Maybe he had to finish fixing up some martinis for—"

He broke off. The cheerful ringing had abruptly ended.

"Hello," he shouted. "Hello? Hello?"

"Good," said Dora, hearing him. "Tell them we're lost."

Wag, wag, concurred Myron, hearing him. Mention that I'd much appreciate a nice open fire.

19

"No one answered," Dick said. "The phone went dead."

"Then why did you say 'hello'?" Dora asked.

"Funny," Dick said. "I could have sworn . . ."

"What, Dickie?"

"It sounded as though someone had snipped the wire."

"Really? What did that sound like?"

"Snip," said Dick.

Their every move watched and appreciated at No. 22 Lola Lane, the three of them set off again on the long, long walk back to where they had left the Rolls, the foggy countryside not having sprung to life in the meanwhile with helpful 24-hours-open service stations.

Eventually, however, the familiar aristocratic outline of the car loomed up and they tumbled thankfully into the front seats. It was then, as she settled down, that Dora noticed the fuel indicator registering empty.

She pointed to it in silent fury.

But Dick's face immediately brightened.

"Now, there," he said, "we have a problem I can deal with."

"You can deal with the problem of having no gas in the middle of countryside that has no gas stations?"

"Certainly."

Dick reached forward. He flipped open the glove compartment. There, beside the box of olives, lay a substantial silver flask. It contained perhaps half a gallon of martini—less a certain amount for previous consumption. Dick took the flask, got out of the car and walked around to the rear (it was rather a long way). He walked back (it was still rather a long way). He got in. He pulled the starter button. The Rolls purred. The Rolls liked martinis as much as its driver!

In the viewing room at No. 22 Benson coughed discreetly.

"I thought he dealt with that rather well, sir," he said.

"Bah," related Lionel Twain.

But even on martinis the going for the Rolls was tough. Peering through the softly swishing windshield wipers at the almost invisible road ahead, Dick at last spotted a road sign looming out of a particularly thick bank of fog. He strained to read it.

VERY THICK FOG AHEAD

Lionel Twain was restored to good humor by the Charlestons' reaction to that particular little joke of his. Neither of them took it well.

"It's at times like these," Dick said viciously, "that I wish Myron were a bloodhound."

"Dickie, please," said Dora, deeply shocked. "You know how sensitive Myron is."

She turned to the rear seat to comfort the poor doggie-woggie.

"Are you sensitive, Myron dear? Myron! Myron? Dick! Dick! Stop the car!"

They jerked to a halt.

"What is it?"

"It's Myron," Dora replied. "We left him outside when we started off again."

"Benson," said Lionel Twain, in the viewing room, "another martini."

"Yes, sir," said Benson, and only right under his breath did he add, "Bah."

"And I think we'll move across to the other channel, Benson."

"Yes, sir."

Click.

Somewhere else in the fog a late 1940s Chevy was driving in the general direction of Lola Lane at a speed hardly greater than that of the Rolls, for all the push and urgency of the young man at the wheel. Though young Willie Wang was all Oriental in appearance, he had none of the calm that ought to go with the ancient wisdom of the East. In fact, in both dress and manner he was an all-American go-getter. Only he was finding it pretty hard to go or to get in fog like this.

By his side, however, sat someone as impassively Oriental as could be, none other than the celebrated Mr. Sidney Wang, solver of dozens of altogether mysterious crimes that had fallen, more or less, within the jurisdiction of the Cataline police force. Only his clothes were not the epitome of Old China, consist-

21

ing as they did of a dark suit of conservative cut, a
good thick topcoat of guaranteed antifog qualities
with a solid black derby to keep the cold from the
all-important head area.

For several miles they had driven, extremely slowly,
in complete silence. But now young Willie Wang
decided it was time to speak, just in time for the listen-
ing audience.

"Some fog, hey, Pop?"

"Drive, please," replied his imperturbable father.
"Have already heard weather report."

"Boy," the unabashed Willie went on, for all the
world as if his revered father had not spoken. "Boy,
it's thick as pea soup. Not a soul around for miles.
Know what I think, Pop?"

Young Willie did not wait to see whether his revered
senior wanted to hear what he thought.

"Perfect place for a murder," he said cheerfully.

In the viewing room Lionel Twain laughed. And
laughed. Benson sighed.

"Conversation like television set on honeymoon,"
said the wonder of the Cataline police force. "Un-
necessary."

"Sorry, Pop."

Short silence.

Very short.

"Gee, I hope these people are going to serve dinner
pretty soon. I'm starving."

"Not surprising," replied the parental voice. "Since
you ate at home one hour ago."

But some sons are born with hides of steel.

"Where are we going, anyway, Pop? And who's
this Mr. Twain who invited you? And what did he
mean by 'dinner and a murder'?"

"Questions like athlete's foot," replied his reverend
sire. "After a while very irritating."

For about five seconds silence descended again inside the old Chevy. Then Sidney Wang spoke.

"Please to stop car."

"Why?" asked young Willie, still peering through
the fog and proceeding at a steady ten miles an hour.
"What's wrong?"

22

"To stop car, please."

Willie brought the Chevy to a halt.

"Please to shut engine off," his enigmatic pa instructed.

"Willie obeyed. In the fogbound night silence descended.

"Listen," Sidney Wang commanded.

"I don't hear nothing," his son replied at once. "What do you hear?"

"Double negative, and a dog," said Sidney Wang.

And, sure enough, through the thick blanket of the fog there could be heard the sharp yapping of a dog.

"Again," said Mr. Wang. "You hear?"

"So it's a dog," Willie replied with a shrug. "So what?"

"Not just any dog," his father said with calm. "Very special bowwow. If not mistaken, dog belongs to Mista Dick Charleston."

Willie, however, was not as impressed with the great detective's brilliance as he might be. But at No. 22, Benson was.

"Most astute, sir," he murmured.

"Bah," said Lionel Twain.

"Who's Dick Charleston?" Willie asked his father.

His question was answered in an altogether unexpected way. From out of a white mound of fog a man's head and shoulders suddenly appeared. They were thrust toward the open window of the old Chevy.

"*I'm* Dick Charleston," said a voice. "Thank you."

The head came in at the window.

"I say," Dick asked, "did you happen to see a little white—Wang!"

"A white Wang?" said Willie, meeting an entirely new concept.

"Good heavens," Dick went on, peering further into the car. "Sidney Wang. What are you doing in this godforsaken spot?"

'No doubt same as you," Sidney Wang replied imperturbably. "Looking for bridge that leads to home of host, Mista Lionel Twain."

"You, too, eh?" Dick said. "Must be important to

23

invite two such eminent detectives . . . I see you've had your hat blocked again."

Wang nodded agreement.

"Must keep good roof on house where brains live. Excuse, please, to introduce Japanese son, Willie."

"Hi," said Willie, very ornately Japanese.

"Japanese?" Dick asked. "But I thought you were . . ."

"Chinese?" Wang completed the sentence. "But of course I am. However, Mrs. Wang and I could never have children. So Willie adopted Number Three Son."

"My pleasure," said Dick. "Well, be careful of this road. It's treacherous."

The old Chevy started up again.

"Treacherous road like fresh mushrooms," sagely observed Sidney Wang. "Must always . . ."

But the Chevy had jerked forward with a muffled roar.

"Idiot," Wang yelled at his son. "Not finish. Wanted to tell him about mushrooms."

"Well," said Lionel Twain, rubbing his hands in glee in the viewing room. "It looks to me as if the great Sidney Wang is going to be in some difficulties when he begins to meet the little surprises we have in store, eh, Benson?"

"Possibly, sir," Benson replied.

And he stuck his nose in the air.

3

Lionel Twain examined the dials on a nearby console connected to the fog machine installed in his grounds. They indicated beyond doubt that the vast quantities of cottonwool-thick mist were still being churned into the air to add to the puny efforts of nature in the San Francisco area. He sighed with pleasure.

"Let's try the Milo Perrier Show," he said to the faithful Benson. "We could get some pretty good laughs there, I bet."

"If you say so, sir," Benson replied.

He leaned forward and clicked a switch. On the screen an inside view of a luxurious Citroën appeared. It was possible to make out, through Nature's inferior fog, that the vehicle was still just within city limits, though its uniformed chauffeur was pushing it along at a rate that should ensure that the genius of the little gray cells, gourmet *extraordinaire* (at that moment munching thoughtfully on a large bar of chocolate), great detective *par excellence,* would get to the old house on time.

But, glimpsing through the thick mist, the faint glow of an occasional neon sign still, the great detective shook his famous egg-shaped head.

"Cannot we go a little faster?" he asked Marcel, his chauffeur.

"I'm sorry, *monsieur*," Marcel answered. "But I can see nothing. This fog is as thick as *bouillabaisse*."

"Nuts," said Perrier sharply.

"I beg your pardon," Marcel said, grappling unsuccessfully with the notion of a fog as thick as nuts. Hazelnuts or peanuts? It was hard to decide.

"Nuts, nuts," Perrier repeated in rage. "There are no nuts in my chocolate. We see a *magasin*—'ow you say?—a shop that advertises it is selling the proper Swiss chocolate, I give you my order and the stupid *imbécile* in the place gives you a raisin bar when I am asking for nuts."

Marcel gave a shrug.

"He did not have any nuts," he answered sulkily.

"The man in the shop?"

"Yes, *monsieur,* that is the *raison* I took the raisin."

"Never mind, never mind," Perrier snapped. "It will not be too long till we are there, and after all, I have been invited to dinner, and a murder. There will be poached salmon with, I think, a *sauce béarnaise.* And then there is here an excellent way of cooking the pigeon—'ow you say?—the squab. It is done in a fashion most tender with . . ."

"But, *monsieur,* there was no mention in the invitation of the menu. How would you know what it is that is going to appear?"

Milo Perrier sighed. Always there are imbeciles.

"No one would send for Milo Perrier, the greatest of detectives," he explained patiently, "all the way across that accursed Atlantic merely to serve him with —'ow you say?—the franks and the beans."

Content with this pronouncement, he sat peering through the windshield ahead. Then suddenly his whole plump body went rigid.

"Stop the car!" he shouted.

"The car?"

"Oui, imbécile, stop the car."

Marcel brought the glossy vehicle to a halt. Around them the white banks of fog curled and settled.

"Turn off the motor," commanded Perrier.

Marcel obeyed.

"What is it, *monsieur?"* he whispered in fright.

"Quiet," whispered Perrier. "Do not move. Do not speak a word. And above all, do not leave the car."

26

And in a twinkling he was gone into the enveloping fog.

"I imagine, sir," said Benson, back in the cosy comfort of the viewing room at Lola Lane, "that *Monsieur* Perrier has had one of those lightning flashes of intuition which so enliven the pages of his chronicles."

"Bah," said Lionel Twain. "There's nothing for him to have any lightning flash of intuition about. They haven't begun to meet my little boxes of tricks yet."

"No, sir."

"No, sir? No, sir? What do you mean 'No, sir' in that damned snide way? What could Perrier be having a flash of intuition about? Eh? Eh? Come on, tell me."

"*Monsieur* Perrier, sir," Benson replied loftily, "was not accustomed, as I am sure you will recall, to tell his Watson, the impenetrably stupid Captain Eastbourne, the full processes of his mind until a convenient moment had arrived in the plot."

Lionel Twain grunted.

"Well, there ain't gonna be no convenient moment in this plot," he said. "Because I'm writing it, see?"

"Yes, sir. Certainly, sir."

"Oh, turn over to the Charlestons again. At least we'll get some decent dialogue there, even if we can hardly expect any decent detection."

Delighted with the neatness of the joke, the seventeenth richest man in the world turned giggling to the screen again.

In the convertible Rolls, still searching the fogbound countryside for the missing Myron, Dick Charleston was beginning to tell Dora about his encounter with the occupants of the battered old 1940s Chevy.

"That was the only detective who ever outsmarted me on a case," he said.

"Well, now, let me guess. Inspector Maigret."

"No, no," Dick said, a little miffed. "Forget it."

"No, I like this. Lew Archer?"

Silence.

"Nero Wolfe?"

27

Cold silence in the car. A wicked chuckle in the viewing room.

"Philip Marlowe?"

Very cold silence in the car. Loud laughter from Lionel Twain.

"Lord Peter Wimsey?"

Freezing silence in the car. Cackles of delight in the viewing room.

"Father Brown?"

"Dr. Fell?"

"Mr. Campion?"

"Ellery Queen?"

"Inspector Ghote of Bombay, even?"

In the viewing room Lionel Twain was rocking to and fro in his chair, tears of mirth streaming down his face.

"Inspector Ghote of Bombay," he repeated. "Inspector Ghote of Bombay. Magnificent. Marvelous."

He turned to Benson.

"Why," he said, "that was the detective in the millionth mystery I threw all the way down the library in sheer exasperation the night that we began all this. Remember? Inspector Ghote, he's the worst of them all. Oh, good girl, Dora, good girl. How that must sting the old smoothie. How that must sting him."

"Shall we try another channel, sir?" Benson said.

Lionel Twain peered at the screen.

"Well, as Charleston seems to have sunk into a complete sulk," he said, "I suppose we might as well. Let's try Diamond. Try Sam Diamond."

Mouth set in rigid disapproval, Benson leaned forward and switched over.

Moving equally slowly through the fog toward that dinner and that promise of a murder the screen showed a battered old T-bird containing two figures. At the wheel there was a man in a trench coat, its collar pulled up high, the wide-brimmed hat above it pulled down low. What could be seen of the face between, sharply intent on getting the big old T-bird through the fog, was handsome though events-battered. Beside the driver a girl could be seen. A blond. All that needed be said of her was: she's been around.

28

And at that moment she was not exactly happy.

"If you ask me, Sam," she was saying bitterly, "this is a wild-goose chase."

"No one asked you, Tess baby," a tough voice shot back.

"Yes, they did," Tess indignantly replied. "You asked me, Sam Diamond. You asked me back there if I thought we were on some wild-goose chase."

"That was then, and this is now and nobody knows what tomorrow will be," the voice said through tight lips, husky and laconic. "That's the way things are, whether we like it or not."

Moved, for all her brassy air of toughness, Tess put her hand over Sam's as it rested on the wheel.

"Oh, Sam," she said. "I worry about you sometimes. I really do."

A crooked smile broke the rugged surface of Sam Diamond's face.

" 'Oh, Sam,' " he mimicked, " 'I worry about you sometimes . . .' That's terrific, angel. How many guys have you told that to?"

"Just you. I swear. You're the only Sam I know."

"Awright," Sam gritted back. "Cut the malarkey. This trip is strictly business with me. Now, what've you got on this Twain guy?"

From her bag Tess extracted a battered cardboard folder. She opened it, shuffled through the half-dozen sheets of paper it contained, picked out one, and began to read.

In the viewing room Lionel Twain leaned forward, his eyes glittering.

"No one knows too much about him," Tess told Sam. "But he's got dough, that's for sure. He bought that house and the land that goes with it for five million. Cash. And all in singles."

"Married?" came the query from between tight lips.

"Six times," Tess replied promptly.

"Fancy that. Where are they now?"

"She's dead."

"She?"

"He kept marrying the same woman," Tess explained. "He was nuts about her."

29

Sam sighed.

"I've been in this business a long time, angel," he said. "And there's one thing I've learned. Never trust a man who marries the same broad six times."

Tess took in this piece of steel-tough wisdom, wide-eyed.

"Any children?" asked the voice from between tight lips.

"One daughter, thirty-two," Tess supplied. "Her name is Irene, but she calls herself Rita. Educated in Switzerland, married a Polish chess player who committed suicide after losing three hundred matches in a row, and none of them to Bobby Fischer."

"I think I read about that," Sam said. "Go on."

"Twain was born in San Francisco in 1905. His mother was a Roman Catholic, his father an orthodox Jew. They were separated two days after the marriage."

"Just like a dame," said the voice out of tight lips. "Don't stop, angel, you're doing fine."

"He was arrested in 1932 in Chicago for selling pornographic Bibles," Tess continued, peering at her notes. "The D.A. couldn't make the charge stick when the church refused to hand over the Bibles. Nothing on him after that till 1946, when he was picked up in El Paso, Texas."

"What was that for, baby?"

"Trying to smuggle a truckload of rich white Americans across the border into Mexico to pick melons. He was sent to Dallas State Hospital for mental observation."

Sam pondered.

In the viewing room Lionel Twain took a sly look at Benson. The butler was nodding benign approval. Twain rubbed his hands together.

"I think we picked ourselves a queer bird, angel," Sam said at last. "But you did your homework good."

Tess looked at him with big eyes suddenly moist.

"Thanks, Sam," she gulped.

"How d'you dig up all this stuff?" Sam said.

"I wrote to Twain and asked him," came the simple reply.

"Good thinking, angel."

In the viewing room Lionel Twain once more burst into cackles of eldritch laughter.

"Well, Benson," he spluttered at last. "What do you think of your ace investigator and his sidekick now? Eh? Eh?"

"Might we see Miss Jessica Marbles, sir?" Benson said.

Icily.

"By all means. Switch over. Switch over."

The vehicle that came up on the screen was approaching San Francisco through the fog from the east. Already it had covered the 4,500 miles from New York at the same steady plod. But it had come much further than that. It was a London taxi.

The driver, a bleary-eyed, walrus-mustached figure in a heavy topcoat humped around his shoulders and with a single silvery translucent drip forever trembling on the end of his potato-shaped, beacon-red nose, was of course alone in the front of the upright vehicle. In the rear, separated from him by a glass partition, there was sitting Miss Jessica Marbles, commanding of visage, straight of back for all her years, tweed-clad from head to foot. Beside her, and fast asleep, there was a shapeless bundle, to which occasionally she gave an investigatory prod as if to make sure that life was still there.

Every now and again she leaned forward and slid open the glass partition an inch or two.

"Driver," she said shortly after transmission had begun, "I hope I shan't have to accuse you of dawdling. Don't think you can expect a tip from me if we are late."

The bleary-eyed figure at the wheel gave a huge sniff that set the dewdrop on his lantern-nose trembling yet more dangerously.

"You'll be there, mum," he muttered, as one who has heard this threat some seven hundred and twenty-two times since Miss Marbles hailed his cab as he was passing Victoria Station back in the British capital some six days before.

31

"I hope so," Miss Marbles answered sharply. "It's not as though the weather's bad or anything."

She looked out of the cab window with pleasure at the rolling banks of white fog. No ardent traveler, she found it a comfort to be reminded of the everyday appearance of her own familiar London streets as seen in her occasional trips up from her Sussex cottage.

"Driver?"

"Yes, mum?"

"Was that a yellow tulip I saw just then?"

The driver did not bother to dangle his dewdrop in the likely direction of the flower. A tulip by the roadside's brim a simple tulip was to him and it was nothing more.

"Yes," said Miss Marbles, with gratified decision. "A yellow tulip. There can be little doubt of it.

'Rosemary is for remembrance
A yellow tulip means hopeless love,
Orchids mean "I await your favors"
Dahlias mean treachery and misrepresentation.'

Yes, a yellow tulip. Ah, my dear. My dear. And it was all such a long time ago."

A trace of a tear—or was it just some condensation from the fog?—came to her eye. She let it lie there for a little, till suddenly a thought struck her and she brushed the fragile drop sharply away.

"Or was it a dahlia?" she asked aloud. "Was that a dahlia?"

"Was it a dahlia?" Lionel Twain asked, kicking his heels in delight. "Did you hear her, Benson? Why, she's incapable of a piece of simple botany, let alone a piece of complex detection. Oh dear, oh dear, oh dear."

"Indeed, sir," murmured Benson.

Viciously.

"Well, let's have some action," Lionel Twain said. "Let's have some action. Go back to Diamond. I could just enjoy a bit of that tough talk between tight lips."

"You don't think, sir, that *Monsieur* Perrier might provide more entertainment? There is the matter of his mysterious errand in the fogbound night, sir."

"I said Diamond, man. And I meant Diamond. Switch over."

"Very good, sir."

The battered old T-bird was making its way slowly but steadily onward.

Slowly but, suddenly, not so steadily.

The motor chugged. Then it grunted. And after a minute the car jerked to a total halt.

"What is it?" Tess asked, a thrill of fear tracing its way across her voice.

Sam Diamond leaned back in his scruffed leather seat.

"Wouldn't you know," he said. "Out of gas."

Lionel Twain chortled.

"I should have done it to all of them," he said.

For a little in the T-bird they sat in silence while the fog tentacles curled lovingly around them, poking and prying at the none-too-well-fitting windows. Then Tess made a tentative suggestion.

"I saw a gas station about five miles back, Sam."

Sam gave her a long, slow appraising look. He bit thoughtfully at his lower lip. Then he made up his mind. He reached over the seat and groped about on the floor at the back. When he straightened up he was holding a very large gas can.

He handed it to Tess.

"I want you to know," he told her softly, "I'll be waitin' for you, baby."

33

4

At last and at last the first of the five cars slowly approaching the big house in its extensive grounds, protected from the vulgar by a swift-flowing stream crossed only by a single bridge, came within reach of the camera ready waiting for it at the border of the estate. It was the 1940s Chevy, conveying the redoubtable Sidney Wang.

The fog here was denser, its wreaths and coils were thicker than anywhere else in all the surrounding countryside. It was as if Nature itself had conspired to protect the grim old house and its every secret (admittedly with some help from Lionel Twain, Esquire). Even the secret that was yet to be: the murder that was promised.

In the viewing room Lionel Twain crouched forward eagerly in his chair.

"Ought to see some fun now, Benson."

"Yes, sir," said Benson.

And crossed his British fingers.

"That's the bridge, Pop," Willie Wang said. "It doesn't look very safe to me."

Fair comment. The bridge looked about as unsafe as a bridge could look, or as that master of the macabre, L. Twain, could manage. It was built of wood, a couple of felled logs that ran along its length visibly getting thinner as they receded into the foggy dark. A few struts ran down from them to the steep bank of the little fast-flowing stream, its dark waters chuckling evilly as if they had spotted the car crawling toward them and expected a meal very, very shortly. Across the two thinning tree trunks, planks were placed, ominous gaps clearly visible between each one. Two of them were skillfully broken, leaving wider gaps above the chuckling black water. Only on one side was there a handrail, so fragile that it would be more of a hindrance than a help to anybody trying to walk across. Grab it and, if L. Twain's calculations were right, it would fall away at your touch and drag you with it into the icy water.

Willie looked at the bridge. He wished he were back home in Cataline. There was central heating in the Wang home, modest though it was. There was a refrigerator, though it groaned horribly at intervals all through the night. But its shelves were well stocked with snacks of this and that in the Chinese manner, and a snack is a mighty comforting thing. There was no television in the Wang home—Sidney Wang considered that television did not exactly fit his image—but there were radios and they could be twiddled until they produced a nice stream of pop music. And pop music could be a very comforting thing.

Much more comforting than thick white fog curling and curling around a 1940s Chevy, thought Willie. Much more comforting than an ancient and decrepit wooden bridge spanning an evil, dark, and chuckling stream.

"Pop, it isn't very safe," he announced with stunning originality.

"One way to find out," replied his father. "Drive across."

Willie sighed. Good Chinese boy obeys parental order without great deal of hooey. So does good Japanese adopted boy. He put the Chevy in gear and crept the heavy old car slowly forward.

"Stop," commanded Sidney Wang.

Good Chinese boy obeyed parental order without great deal of hooey, especially as parental order suited him very well.

"Good," said Sidney Wang. In a trice he was out of the Chevy and on the solid roadway.

36

"Now drive," he said.

Back in the viewing room Benson ventured a discreet cough.

"Rather astute, sir, I thought," he said.

"You've no business to think," Lionel Twain snapped back. "You're a butler, aren't you? Well, butler, damn you, butler."

"Yes, sir," said Benson.

On the screen Willie was putting the old Chevy into bottom gear. Slowly, slowly he eased the heavy old car forward toward the slimy old tumbledown bridge. Japanese boy was plainly hoping and hoping Chinese father would rescind stupid order which had to be obeyed without a great deal of hooey.

He opened the car window wide.

"Good thinking, sir, since the prospect must loom large of the car lying on its side in the icy waters of your evil and chuckling stream," Benson remarked.

Lionel Twain made no reply.

Willie put his Japanese ear as close to the window as possible, plainly hoping to catch sound of Chinese parent rescinding stupid order that had to be obeyed without great deal of hooey.

The foggy night was very, very silent.

The wheels of the Chevy touched the first plank of the bridge. The whole structure shook as if it were entirely built of pairs of castanets. The car mounted the first plank. Its wheels seemed to hold it down a little and the frenzied castanet clicking all along the length of the slimy old bridge calmed down. The wheels touched the second plank. Castanets broke out in a new spasm of wild Spanish-dancer clicking. The wheels held down the second plank. Castanet music went into a diminuendo. Followed at once by a crescendo as the wheels butted up against the third plank. Diminuendo followed, then crescendo. But with the whole car on the bridge its weight seemed to hold the entire structure firmly down.

"A small miscalculation, sir?" Benson asked.

"Not at all, not at all," Lionel Twain snarled.

Now instead of castanet music there were oboes,

37

bassoons, trombones, and an occasional high-pitched clarinet squeak.

Willie looked as if he was thinking that pop music from radio in safe Chinese home was much preferable.

The car inched forward, its motor running so slowly that not only could the groans and grunts of the bridge be clearly heard but from under them another sound, the evil chuckling of the stream below.

Suddenly Willie could take the strain no more. He put his foot hard down on the accelerator, making the old car leap forward. No doubt it had been thinking that a cold chuckling stream was no place for an old Chevy that had served a distinguished Chinese detective for many a year.

The bridge protested. No doubt it had had other ideas altogether from the old Chevy. Doubtless it thought its great moment had come at last. After many and many a year of undistinguished existence, with those damned insects always eating its legs, it was about to go out in a blaze of glory, to be the end of a distinguished Chinese detective. (Well, how can a bridge tell that a distinguished Chinese detective has had the distinguished common sense to get out of a heavy old Chevy before vehicle is set on decrepit old bridge?) And now the damned Chevy was trying its best to deprive a good old honest decrepit bridge of its moment of glory. Protest. Protest.

Sigh.

The heavy old Chevy was safe on the other side. Foiled again.

"Oh, very good, sir," said Benson.

"Bah," said Lionel Twain.

On the far side, on very, very nice, very, very firm ground, Willie shut down the Chevy's motor and leaned out of the window.

"I made it, Pop! I made it!" he called out cheerfully.

He could no longer see his distinguished Chinese father for the denseness of the fog and the deepness of the dark. But a voice called cheerfully back.

"Good boy. Now come back and get adopted father."

In the viewing room Lionel Twain dug Benson in the ribs, not a thing you do with impunity to a British butler, not unless you are at least the nineteenth richest man in the world.

"One cannot win them all, sir," Benson said, wincing a little. "And in any case the car may get across safely with both of them in it."

"Of course it will, you fool," Lionel Twain answered with a fearful grin. "Do you think I wanted to drown them before I've really begun? Now, turn over to someone else. Let's see another of them making a fool of himself."

"Very well, sir," said Benson. "Shall we try *Monsieur* Perrier?"

"We shall not. Get Charleston."

In the Rolls convertible, making its way still at no great speed toward No. 22, all appeared to be gaiety once more. Myron had rejoined the fold, and Dick Charleston was lifting his voice in song.

> "If a body meets a body
> Comin' through the rye
> Will somebody find a body
> Will somebody die?"

The last note died away richly.

"Oh, he won't sing for long," Lionel Twain said, rubbing his lily-white hands.

"But he does sing nicely, sir," Benson ventured.

"Nicely? Nicely? What a damned British expression."

"Yes, sir," said Benson.

"You're in a chipper mood, I must say," commented Dora.

"I am, aren't I?" Dick answered blithely. "And do you know why that is, darling?"

"No, darling, I do not know why that is."

"I smell crime in the air."

"I'm not surprised," Dora came sharply back. "You just ran over a small animal."

Lionel Twain drummed his feet on the floor beneath him in sheer delight.

"Great detective, great detective," he gasped, his eyes streaming.

39

"Anyone can have a small motoring accident, sir," Benson said.

In the Rolls Dick Charleston seemed to be of the same opinion.

"Eerie shadows round here," he said after a little, in a defensive tone. "I could have sworn I saw someone on foot up ahead just now, till the fog came back."

Dora peered out at the surrounding countryside. Dark shapes loomed. Fog swirled.

"These woods give me the creeps," she said. "They remind me of the moors of Scotland."

"No, no, darling," Dick corrected her hastily. "The Moores have a beach house. It's the Kents who have the place in the woods."

"The Moores," said Dora icily, as icily as the creeping fog, "the Moores are next to the Kents in the woods. They moved there last winter."

"I didn't know that," Dick said. "I thought the Moores were—"

His voice came to a sudden stop.

"Good grief"

"A figure had risen up right in front of the Rolls, appearing suddenly out of the bank of fog, dark, looming, menacing. And almost right in front of the car.

Dick jammed his foot on the brake. All those little notions which Mr. Rolls and Mr. Royce had for their cars back in craftsmanlike old England came into force. The big vehicle pulled to a swift and silent halt.

But there was a terrible scream from just ahead. The figure that had so suddenly come out of the mist whirled and flung out an arm. There was a terrible hollow bonking sound.

Dick leaned out of the hastily wound-down window.

"Are you all right?" he asked into the fog.

No answer.

Dora laid a hand on his arm, reassuring him.

"Hello," he called again. "Are you all right?"

Still no answer.

Dick fumbled for the door catch. Had a death

occurred? Was this perhaps the murder that the invitation spoke of? Murder by car? The victim suddenly thrown in front of the detective's very own vehicle?

"Hello there?"

But then, before he had time to step down into the road, the figure staggered out of the dark and fog into the light coming from the fog lamps. It was a girl. She was blond. All that it was necessary to say of her was that she'd been around.

She was staggering, and no wonder. She had picked up once more the heavy can of gas she had been lugging toward the stalled T-bird somewhere up ahead on the foggy road.

"I still have about three miles to go back to my car," she said in answer to Dick's instant apologies. "Thank goodness you saw me when you did."

Dick agreed. "I wouldn't want blood on my hands twice tonight."

He restarted the Rolls.

"I'm glad you're all right," he said. "Keep to the side of the road."

He gave her a cheery wave. In a moment the fog swallowed up the big car just like a gourmet slipping down an oyster.

Benson asked himself whether his master was in danger of death by apoplexy. Seldom had he seen anyone laugh so much. A few pained thoughts crossed his mind.

"Well, sir," he said, when at last the laughing had quietened enough to make rational conversation a possibility. "Well, sir, you cannot deny that Mr. Charleston preserves his good manners, whatever the circumstances."

"Good manners? Good manners to leave that poor dumb blond stranded in the middle of all that fog?"

"I meant, sir, that he bade the lady good-bye in the most pleasant of ways. And, besides, there wouldn't be quite so much fog, sir, if it wasn't for your machine."

"Quite so, Benson. Quite so. And it's getting them

into a rare state, my fog. Did you ever see such a lot of buffoons?"

"That is as may be, sir. But I observe that one of the parties has arrived outside the house—despite your fog and your bridge and your emptied petrol tanks."

"Petrol, Benson? What's petrol, in heaven's name?"

"Petrol, sir, is the correct word for gasoline. Or what some people in this country refer to as gas."

Benson, his face a mask, turned his attention to the screen.

In front of the looming bulk of the old house, crowned and pinnacled by the fog, an old 1940s Chevy could be seen just pulling up. As it did so, Sidney Wang thrust his head cautiously out of the window and surveyed what he could see of the building for fog. It was precious little. Only an arch with above it in large black figures the house number, then farther back an impression of high towering walls. If there were windows, they must be closely shuttered. Not a glimmer of light appeared anywhere.

Willie got out of the car, lugging with him a fat old suitcase. Together he and his father approached the broad flight of steps going up to the door, Wang's eyes darting from side to side as if, going through his head like a tape loop, were the words "You are cordially invited to dinner . . . and a murder."

But, standing where he was, the top of the towering old house was almost lost to his view in the dense-wrapping fog. And he ought to have looked up. He really ought. For his own sake.

Because on the parapet, high, high above the ground, a huge stone statue, one of half a dozen ornamenting the front of the mansion, was being at that very instant maneuvered forward by a dutiful Benson toward the edge. Quarter-inch by quarter-inch.

Push and pause. Push and pause. Benson, however reluctant, worked hard to shift the massive piece of stone, carved into an unlikely representation of the figure of Justice, a pair of scales in one hand (just noticably tipped to one side) and in the other a sword

42

held upright and with the end broken off. Around its face, which would appear to be that of a drunken lady of late middle age, was tied a stone bandage blotting out the eyes.

And bit by bit, quarter-inch by quarter-inch the whole caboodle got nearer and nearer to toppling point.

Meanwhile, directly below, the cautious Wang surveyed the high-pointed door in front of him, and even the stone steps up to it. with the very greatest of care. A number of appropriate Chinese proverbs rolled slowly through his head.

Above, in the fog, Benson pushed and pushed. A little British sweat beaded his brow and even more collected inside the pair of white gloves he had donned on the orders of his master. Somebody reads too many damned detective stories.

Push. Push. Pant. Push. Push.

Our slightly drunken middle-aged lady friend with the stone bandage around her eyes was beginning to feel more than a little queasy, so it would seem. Why else was she beginning to topple forward like that?

Down below on the steps the two Wangs stood side by side, shoulder to shoulder.

Then suddenly august father spoke.

"Stop!"

"Huh?" said un-august son.

"Do not move," Wang Senior barked. "Something wrong here."

"What is it, Pop?"

"Do as I say," Wang replied. "Do not ask questions. When I tell you jump, jump. One . . ."

Our drunken lady friend rocked slowly back up on the parapet above, as if she had decided that tonight after all was not a very good time to see whether she could fly. The gloved hands pushed furiously. The lady seemed to think that, no, perhaps tonight was quite a good night to try a flip around the countryside. The fog might help. Be kind of thicker, you know?

She began to lunge forward again.

Down on the steps directly below it was "Two."

"Yes, the lady had definitely decided on flying. And it was too late now to change her mind—whatever anybody says about a woman's privilege.

Down on the steps it was "Three."

5

Through the dark and foggy air a certain slightly drunken middle-aged lady, carrying in one outstretched hand a pair of scales (slightly tilted) and in the other an upright sword (with its end broken), convinced that fog had particularly good supportive qualities, attempted to fly. But, since she happened to be made of solid stone and to weigh close on half a ton, her flying was conducted feet first.

And though, certainly, she proceeded through the air at a great and ever-increasing rate (see the experiments of one Galileo at the Leaning Tower of Pisa) her trajectory was hardly what any unbiased observer would call flight, since it was straight downward toward the ground.

And down on the ground, on the broad flight of steps leading up to the front door of No. 22 Lola Lane where Sidney Wang, renowned Chinese detective, and Willie Wang, unrenowned adopted Number Three son, were shoulder to shoulder, it was "Jump."

Sidney Wang himself jumped to the right, and far. Willie, ever mindful of the need to obey parental orders without great deal of hooey, jumped to the left, if possible even farther than distinguished, but portly, father.

The slightly drunken lady with the sword and the scales arrived exactly between them. With an almighty crash.

45

As its echoes died away into the surrounding fog, a long silence settled in. At last Willie broke it.

"Holy Shanghai!" he exclaimed. "Nice counting, Pop. But how did you know?"

"Look there," his father said, pointing.

And there, slightly obscured by a thick powdering of stone lady, but clear enough to be seen when peered at, were the chalked outlines of two pairs of feet.

"Even had correct shoe sizes," Wang commented. "Someone has gone to great trouble to make welcome guests not so welcome."

He gave a little shrug.

"Ring bell, please," he said to Willie.

Willie looked at him as if little pink man had suddenly begun to dance all around the edge of his black derby.

"Are you nuts, Pop?" he asked. "Someone just tried to kill us."

"Should make exciting visit, yes?" his father answered, not a bit put out. "Ring bell, please."

Willie stepped carefully through the mound of rubble representing a certain lady who used to stand on a parapet holding a sword with a broken tip and a pair of scales. (How did they get tipped to one side, anyhow? Damned if she can remember. Maybe a bird sat in one pan. Maybe it laid an egg in it. A lead egg.) He approached a large iron handle with letters just above it in black wrought iron spelling out B-E-L. (Accidents will happen.)

"Well, sir," said Benson in the air-conditioned comfort of the viewing room, "you certainly must hand it to Sidney Wang. Imperturbable is the word I should use."

"A butler's no business using words like that," growled Lionel Twain.

"Indeed, sir. But nevertheless you would agree that Mr. Wang's handling of the situation would be hard to beat."

Lionel Twain swung around from the TV screen with a look of impish triumph.

"Hard to beat," he said scornfully. "It was no more

46

than I predicted of him. I didn't want my fox shot before it had even gotten into the stadium."

"I think, sir," said Benson, "that we are getting our sporting metaphors just a little confused. Foxhunting is not generally conducted in stadia, not where I come from, anyway."

"Stadia," said Lionel Twain with contempt.

And he would have added a few other comments on butlers who speak like that. Only Benson spotted some action on the screen.

"He's just going to pull the bell, sir," he interrupted, with a trace of excitement, even.

Lionel Twain chuckled.

"Let's see how your imperturbable Sidney Wang copes with this," he said.

Willie Wang gave the iron bell handle a good hard tug.

From inside the towering old pile in front of him there came echoing and ringing in the dark foggy night the most appalling scream. A scream of pure unalloyed terror, and a woman's scream, too, no doubt about that.

"Holy cow!" Willie exclaimed urgently. "They're killing someone in there."

Sweat stood on his brow. His eyes took on a look of urgent pleading.

"Let's break the door down, Pop," he begged.

He turned and squared his shoulder to the thick oak door, though it was clear that it would take more than the battering he could give it to break it open. But, if this is all he can do, he is ready to do it. That scream echoes in his mind, for all the quiet beyond the door now.

"Calm yourself, please," his father said, holding up his hand in a warning gesture.

"But, Pop . . . But, Pop, you heard that scream."

"You heard scream," replied Sidney Wang, putting all the emphasis on the "you."

He shook his head pityingly.

"More experienced ears heard doorbell," he said.

"Oh, well played, sir, well played," Benson was unable to help himself exclaiming as Sidney Wang's

47

bland statement came through the loudspeakers above.

"Benson, this is not a bloody cricket game."

"It is more usual to say 'match,' sir. A cricket match. And nor does one generally, in good society, precede the term with the expletive 'bloody.' "

Lionel Twain swung around in his chair. It was one of those executive-type chairs designed for dramatic swinging around in.

"But, Benson," he said, an evil leer splitting his face from ear to ear, "this is not good society. Nor is it a cricket *game*. It is a personal matter between myself and these goons who've spoiled every pleasant hour of relaxation that I ever had. Is that understood?"

"Perfectly, sir," said Benson.

"Then will you get into that lift and scoot down to that front door and get the hell on with playing your part?"

"Yes, sir."

"And Benson."

"Sir?"

"You've forgotten your white cane—and your shades."

"Thank you, sir. Most remiss of me, I'm sure."

Lionel Twain turned back to his screen.

"Sometimes," he muttered, "I even get to feel that guy wants to help the goons."

Down at the threshold of the huge old house the great iron-studded oak door creakingly swung open.

Sidney Wang and Number Three Son were confronted by Mr. Twain's confidential butler, in dark glasses and carrying a white stick. Willie goggled. Imperturbable Oriental father remained imperturbable and Oriental.

"Good evening," the butler said in a soft and deferential British voice. "We have been expecting you."

"But in what condition?" Wang asked sharply. "Roof in need of repair."

"Indeed?" replied the butler, with proper British aplomb. "I'm afraid the house is rather falling apart."

He stood on the threshold, a curious, even menacing

48

figure in his black jacket, with the thin white cane dangling from one wrist and those inscrutable dark glasses hiding his eyes. And he made no move whatsoever to let the Wangs past.

At last the Chinese detective spoke.

"May we come in?"

The butler gave a little start.

"I'm so sorry," he said. "I thought you were in. You are Mr. and Mrs. Charleston?"

Willie looked at his portly Oriental father in some astonishment. Mr. Charleston? Well, okay, anybody can make a mistake, and perhaps Charleston could be an old Oriental name. But Mrs. Charleston? Mrs.? And which of them was the guy thinking it was?

"Not quite Mista and Missis Charleston," his father explained, imperturbably. "I am Inspector Wang of Cataline police. This adopted son, Willie."

"Ah, yes, indeed, sir," the butler murmured.

But at least he stepped aside and allowed them into the house.

It was an extraordinary sight that met their eyes. The big door let straight into the Great Hallway of the mansion. It was long enough to put a swimming pool in, dark, gloomy, and mysterious. High on the walls hung the heads of slain stags, punctuated by an occasional tiger. In nooks and corners stood old suits of armor, looking as if there were eyes inside them, watching eyes. Near these, fastened to the walls, were arrangements of various weapons, swords, old pistols, pikes, knobkerries. Death-dealing weapons.

The two Wangs stared and shivered. Nor was that only because the huge old barn of a room was damned cold, though it certainly ought to have been that, considering how much it had cost Lionel Twain to have ice-cooled drafts blown through it.

"I trust you had a pleasant journey, sir," the butler said, bending courteously to address Sidney Wang, and succeeding in pointing himself in almost precisely the totally wrong direction.

"Though I am afraid," he went on, with that British politeness that is often a bit too much of a good thing.

49

"I'm afraid the storm will have dreadfully inconvenienced you."

The storm? Willie Wang, remembering the hours he had driven through that still, blanketing, and silent fog, wondered what on earth this kooky guy could mean. Until he happened to look at one of the tall windows of the long hall.

And saw lightning flashing, accompanied by long rolls of thunder and by the insistent demoniacal tattoo of rain on the panes.

Evidently his father, too, had taken note of these somewhat extraordinary meteorological conditions. Because he turned from the windows to look back out of the still half-open tall front door. Where outside fog rolled and heaved, just as it had done all the way from the city.

"Strange weather," he commented. "Storm only outside when inside."

"Oh, that," the butler said carelessly, giving his favorite Chinese detective a quick wink. "That's just one of Mr. Twain's little toys. An electronic device. Mr. Twain, as you will soon discover, prefers his atmosphere . . ."

He searched for the word.

"Prefers his atmosphere . . . murky."

Willie Wang looked at his father. His father looked imperturbable.

"One moment while I close the door, please," Benson added.

He went back to it, waving his cane till it made contact. Then with his free hand he swung the door firmly—till it came to rest, wide open.

"Now," he said, apparently satisfied, "if you would be so good as to follow me, I shall show you to your room."

He set off along the hall and up the huge distant stairway that wound majestically into the higher regions of the old mansion. The two newcomers followed in silence along a tall and diabolically drafty corridor. Blank and firmly shut doors to either side confronted them like sentinels. Shadows lurked.

Suddenly from behind a door they had just passed

came a deep and ferocious growl, the growl of nothing less than a wolfhound.

Above, Lionel Twain snapped off the button and awaited results.

"What is that, please?" Sidney Wang inquired sedately.

"That?" answered the butler with just the merest hint of an encouraging smile. "It's nothing, sir. Just the cat."

"That is cat?" Wang asked, a little astonished. "You feed cat on dog food?"

"I'm afraid he's a very angry cat, sir," the butler replied, at his most suavely British. "Mr. Twain had him—er—seen to, and he didn't want to be."

"Bah," said Lionel Twain up above. "The guy's cheating. Willie should at least have fainted."

In silence, Sidney Wang pondering and Willie Wang hardly daring to let himself think, let alone ponder, they went farther along the shadow-filled, draft-whistling corridor. At last they halted at one of the blank-looking doors.

Benson opened it in the grand manner. The room inside was pitch-black.

With a slight bow Benson ushered Sidney Wang forward, and Sidney Wang, who was brought up on true Oriental politeness, served with noodles for breakfast, walked boldly in.

There was a devastating crash as if half a dozen brooms had descended onto half a dozen empty metal pails.

Half a dozen brooms had descended onto half a dozen empty metal pails. Wang emerged.

"Very nice broom closet," he remarked gently. "But very difficult for sleep."

"The broom closet," murmured the butler, in apparent surprise. "I am so sorry, sir. I must have 'gotten' myself, as you say in this country, turned the wrong way around."

An American word. It was Benson's tribute to Wang's calm in face of the newest of Lionel Twain's little tricks. He dared do no more.

"Yes, sir," he went on, "I usually come up here

51

by the back stairs. That put me facing the wrong direction. Your room is doubtless here, sir. Just opposite."

"Big houses like man married to fat woman," Wang reassured him. "Difficult to get around."

Willie shook his head wonderingly.

"Boy, it's a cold house," he said.

Benson's face took on a fleeting look of dismay. Too bad, he thought, that the boy should play into into his master's hands. Ah, well . . .

"I've taken care of that, sir," he said smoothly. "You'll find a nice, cosy fire in your room."

He threw open the door. There *was* a nice, cosy fire in the room. It was blazing in the big double bed, instantly ignited at the touch of a switch upstairs. Wang and Willie rushed in and began tugging off the bedclothes.

"Dinner will be at eight," Benson announced from the door. "Mr. Twain prefers that you dress."

He closed the door on the Wangs, stepped swiftly into the black broom closet, went through the concealed door in its rear, and in three seconds had shot up in the lift there to the top of the house and his master's presence.

Lionel Twain did not look in a good humor.

"Benson," he said, mean as a monkey, "you're helping these guys. I don't know what you're doing, but you're giving them hand signals or something."

Benson looked offended, loftily offended.

"At home, sir," he said, "one is taught that there is nothing so despicable as not to play fair."

"And that's why you always lose," Lionel Twain pounced in with glee. "And you're going to lose this time, Benson, I promise you."

"That is as may be, sir," Benson replied.

He allowed his thoughts to dwell fondly on Sidney Wang and the calmly astute way he had dealt with things up to now. Why, he was still every bit as good as he had been even in his first films.

"They got that fire out?" Lionel Twain asked maliciously. "I don't want the whole house burned down, you know."

"I have no doubt, sir, that a little elementary fire drill is well within Sidney Wang's capabilities. And I would beg to draw your attention to the hallway monitor, sir. The Charlestons appear to be entering. I left the door open as you instructed, sir."

"Hm," said Lionel Twain, turning to the correct screen.

"It would seem, sir," Benson added, with hardly a hint of triumph, "that Mr. Charleston has dealt with the matter of the falling statue of Eros, as found at Piccadilly Circus, London, with exemplary coolness."

And, sure enough, on the monitor screen from the hallway it was clear that no more than a powdery dusting of stone lay on Dick Charleston's elegant shoulders.

Dora, however, was slumped on a low armchair in a half faint with Dick holding to her lips a glass containing the last dregs of the martini, prudently held back from the lip-licking Rolls.

"Drink this, darling," he was saying. "You'll feel better in a minute."

Dora took a shaky sip.

"If Myron hadn't barked," she said, a little wildly, "we never would have seen that statue falling. What was it? Eros?"

"Eros it was, darling. The god of love. But I don't think it was meant to kill us. "It was meant as a warning. Someone is trying to frighten us."

"Oh, very well played, sir, very well played," murmured Benson.

He ventured on a burst of quiet clapping.

"You know, sir," he said to Lionel Twain, "I wouldn't be at all surprised if Mr. Charleston solves the murder mystery."

"Well, I would," Lionel Twain snapped back. "I'd be surprised if that twister solved his way through till dinnertime."

Benson gave a superior smile. And generations of British butlers had made Benson's superior smile so superior that strong employers had been known to lie down on the floor and weep when they met it.

But Lionel Twain was made of sterner stuff. It had

got him to be seventeenth richest man in the world, and it wasn't going to let him be smiled down by a Benson.

"Get down to that hallway," he barked. "And this time, no funny tricks."

"A British butler does not play funny tricks, sir. And I would advise you to watch the Citroën."

But all the same, Benson was frowning hard as he turned to the express lift, though, equally, Lionel Twain made no attempt to watch the Perrier channel rather than the Charleston one.

Two seconds later, Dick Charleston tapped Dora gently on the shoulder.

"Up there, Dora," he said quietly. "Look."

She followed the direction of his gaze toward the distant staircase. Down the wide stairs, *tap, tap, tap-tap-tap,* was coming a figure dressed in short black jacket, striped trousers, and dark glasses, and feeling his way forward with the aid of a thin white cane.

"A blind butler?" Dick whispered.

Dora clutched his arm.

"Dickie," she said, her voice rising in urgency, "whatever you do, don't let him park the car."

The butler advanced toward them. But no sooner had he arrived than Myron decided he ought to put in a word on his own behalf. He let loose two or three angry barks, to see what would happen.

He got an unexpected reaction.

"Don't mind him, ma'am," Benson said to Dora (more or less). "That's just the cat."

He led the three of them off toward the stairs.

"We . . . er . . . left a case in the trunk of the car," Dora said tentatively.

"I'll get it later, ma'am," Benson replied, "when I park the car."

6

Dora Charleston's look of absolute dismay at Benson's bland and blind assurance that he would see to the parking of that very costly Rolls convertible was ample reward for Lionel Twain, sitting with his little twinkle toes tucked well under him, watching every move of the Charlestons' arrival.

Nothing like the prospect of a few really deep and long gashes in cherished paintwork to sow the seeds of marital disharmony, he thought. Why, within an hour we'll have this cosy couple really at each other's throats. Then we'll see how clever Dick Charleston is when it comes to solving a truly baffling murder, let alone those few other little surprises I have up my sleeve.

Always provided, he went on, that Benson doesn't get up to any tricks. A butler ought to be loyal. And a British butler ought to be more loyal than that. What did they have a queen for, if it wasn't to teach them how to be loyal?

A sudden expresson of grim doubt on his face, he turned back to his screen.

In the upstairs corridor Dick, Dora, and Myron were following the blind Benson toward the room that had been prepared for them. And that was some preparation.

"Not many people come to the manor nowadays," Benson said. "It's nice to hear guests again."

"Oh, thank you," Dora answered, radiating charm. "Thank you . . . er?"

"Benson, mum," the butler supplied.

"Thank you, Benson."

"Bensonmum," the butler corrected her, sticking strictly to the dialogue his master had written for the occasion, despite all inner doubts about exactly how many laughs it was good for. "My name is Bensonmum. Jamessir Bensonmum."

"Jamessir?" queried Dick.

"Yes, sir."

"Jamessir Bensonmum?" Dick asked, hardly able to believe his sophisticated ears.

"Yes, sir," said Bensonmum, firmly keeping to those rules.

"How odd," Dick said.

"My father's name, sir," replied Bensonmum, quick as a flash, seeing the opportunity for a little improving ad-libbing.

"What was your father's name?"

"How-ard, sir, How-ard Bensonmum."

"Your father was How Odd Bensonmum?" Dick asked, struggling.

"Well, sir," Bensonmum came in quickly, "I suppose by most standards my father was very odd."

Dick Charleston moaned.

Upstairs, Lionel Twain forgave Benson everything. If the Charlestons were not reeling on the ropes by now, it was certainly no fault of the British. "Your father was How Odd?" "By most standards very odd." Why, the joke was worthy of his own wit. It really was.

"Here we are," Benson (or Bensonmum) said. "The late Mrs. Twain's room. She died in here."

He put a good deal of satisfaction in the words. Smiling happily, he then took from his pocket a ring with dozens and dozens of keys and with slowly feeling fingers began to search through them.

"She died in here?" Dora asked, filling in the awkward pause.

"Yes, mum," Benson answered, full to the ears with gloom.

"Oh, dear."

"Died of what?" Dick asked with undisturbed calm.

"She murdered herself, sir," Benson replied, giving Dick full marks. "Murdered herself in her sleep."

"You mean suicide?"

"Oh, no, sir. It was murder all right. Mrs. Twain hated herself."

Benson fumbled through another dozen or so keys.

"Mr. Twain loved her very much, sir," he added in a deeply sepulchral voice. "He's kept her room just as it was the night she died nine years ago."

He swept open the door.

Cobwebs lay thick over every inch of the room that was revealed, joining bed to chair, chair to wash-basin, washbasin to fireplace in great gray loops everywhere. And dust. Dust rested in a heavy layer on every square inch where dust could find anywhere to lay its weary head.

Suddenly, at the unexpected opening of the door after only some nine years, a mouse shot out from under a chair and headed straight across the room for the bed. Dora screamed.

"Ah, the doorbell," said Benson, quick as a flash. He turned to go.

"That," Dick said, "was Mrs. Charleston."

"I thought she was up here with us," Benson replied, hamming his part for every penny that it was worth.

"I *am* up here," Dora said. "And what's more, I won't stay in this horribly filthy room."

"Filthy?" Benson asked in great astonishment.

He shrugged.

"Very well, ma'am, I'll attend to it during dinner."

"Thank you, Bensonsir," Dick said.

"Mum," said Benson.

"What?"

"Bensonmum, sir. Ma'am."

He turned and tapped his way out of the door. Dick rapidly closed it atfer him.

Lionel Twain swiveled around in his chair as, three seconds later, Benson emerged from the secret ex-

57

press lift into the viewing room right at the top of the old house.

"Benson," he said, "I wish to pay tribute to you. You handled that magnificently. Those two won't know which way to turn."

"Thank you, sir," Benson murmured. "I'm afraid that you may be right."

"Afraid?"

Lionel Twain lost his look of benign kindliness in one instant.

"Listen, Benson," he said, "these are rats we have in our rat-run. Understand that. They've made my life a misery for years. They've made millions of innocent people suffer. And now they're getting a taste of their own medicine."

Benson sighed.

"As you say, sir. But nevertheless I must confess to having received a lot of pleasure from their exploits. I mean, sir, what a delightful rapport there always is between Mr. and Mrs. Charleston. And then he is so acute, too. Sir, it gives me shivers of delight at times. Sheer shivers, sir."

"Sheer shivers, bah. Acute? Why, Dick Charleston's about as acute as a blunt knitting needle. Look at him now. Look at him. I'll bet he's doing no more than feebly consoling that wretched wife of his for all those cobwebs and all that dust. Look at him."

He swung his chair round to the TV monitor and jabbed a switch.

"Baking flour," came Dick Charleston's voice.

"What?" said Dora.

"This dust is baking flour. And those cobwebs—"

Dick peered at a choice example closely.

"—are candied sugar. All recently and carefully placed here for the sole purpose of frightening us out of our wits."

Benson turned away and busied himself fixing a martini so as to hide the smile he could not keep off his face.

Below, Dick blew enough flour off a corner of the bed to be able to sit.

"By why?" he asked aloud. "Why? What's Twain's game?"

"Whatever it is," Dora announced firmly, "I don't want to play. Not with a mouse under our bed."

Dick smiled at her indulgently and reached under the bed.

Up above, Benson, who had recovered enough to turn to the screen again, crossed his fingers.

"A mouse, darling?" Dick asked. "Or a mechanical toy?"

He pulled his hand out, closely wrapped around a small furry object so that only a pair of bright button eyes and two little velvet ears were visible.

He brushed a place on the bed clear for Dora with his other hand. She went and sat beside him.

"A statue that just misses us," Dick said meditatively. "A doorbell that screams. A blind butler. A phony rainstorm. And candied cobwebs. Surely Twain can't hope to frighten two such experienced detectives as Wang and myself with such tricks. And yet he——"

Suddenly he broke off. An expression of horror planted itself on his face.

"What is it, Dick?"

"The mouse. It's real."

He dropped the little rodent to the floor, shivering with disgust and wiping his hands furiously on his coat.

Lionel Twain's laughter was painful to hear. Benson tried to think of other things—the queen, Shakespeare, village greens, lukewarm beer—but nothing much helped. The truth was too much for him. His hero was, after all, afraid of a mouse.

"I think, sir," he said, "that I had better go and see to the preparations for dinner. After all, one has a certain reputation to keep up."

Lionel Twain looked at him, his face expressionless.

"Yes, Benson, yes," he said. "Go and see to the dinner by all means. You have your reputation."

Benson turned and glided toward the lift. He was pretty proud of the way he glided.

"And, Benson," Lionel Twain called after him as the lift door began to close, "I've arranged for some help for you. Thought you might welcome it, in view of your reputation."

But only when the lift door was tightly closed did he kick up his heels in delight and allow himself a giggle that would have wound nicely three times around the Empire State Building.

British butlers, he said to himself. British butlers and their reputations. And their disloyalties. Well, Master Benson's got a few surprises coming that even he doesn't know about.

Leanig forward, he opened a small concealed panel beside his battery of TV monitors to reveal yet another screen. It showed, in full color, the kitchen of the old house.

Benson, blind butler shades fully in place, was making his way through familiar territory at speed. Until he discovered the arrival of his help. But bumping into her. She made no comment at this abrupt introduction, and nose-to-nose they stood in front of each other under the happy gaze of Lionel Twain far above.

"Who are you?" Benson asked.

No reply.

Benson exetnded his hands and began feeling at the face so close to his. Satisfied at last as to what that face looked like, his hands moved down to the neck, to the shoulders, to the small of the back, to . . .

A sudden startled look appeared on the face of the silent victim of the feelies.

"Ah," Benson said at last, "you must be the new kitchenmaid. I hope you can cook."

But even his breaking into speech produced no reply from the girl.

"Answer me," Benson said sharply. "Speak up."

But all that happened was that the girl extracted a sheet of paper from the pocket of her dress and held it up in front of the blind butler's eyes. It read: "My name is Yetta. I cannot speak or hear."

"What's that?" Benson said querulously. "I can't hear you."

He cocked his head to make out what his newly arrived helper was saying. But still no signals came in.

"Well, never mind," he said at last, with a shrug. "There'll be ten for dinner. Here's the menu."

He reached out to the big dresser nearby, felt along it till he hit on a large card and handed it to Yetta. She peered at it, and then dipped into another pocket and produced a second note. It read: "I am new to this country. I cannot read English. This note was written for me. (Signed) Acme Letter Writing Service."

"Is that understood?" blind-as-a-bat Benson said forcefully. "Dinner will be at eight. When I want you, that bell on the wall will ring three times."

He turned away.

"All right," he said, "get to work."

He pointed with his cane in the general direction of the stove. But the cane, more or less, indicated a chair drawn up to the big kitchen table. Obediently Yetta went to it, pulled it out, and sat down. Benson left, satisfied that down in the kitchen department all was well.

Lionel Twain awaited his return to the viewing room with carefully concealed pleasure. Yetta was going to provide one or two shocks for Benson before the day was done. And serve him right. Daring to see anything in those old frauds that were getting their comeuppance at last. Well, he'd learn.

"Come in, come in, Benson," he said as the lift door swished open. "You're just in time for the Milo Perrier Show. Daresay it'll be even funnier than the Dick and Dora Charleston Show."

"I shall be interested to discover the exact nature of *Monsieur* Perrier's secret mission, sir," Benson said.

Lionel Twain noted with pleasure that for all the bravado of the words he still seemed a little worried. No doubt he wasn't all that happy about dinner, and his reputation.

"Look," he said, "look. They're just coming in."

Benson turned to the screen.

"Well, sir," he observed, "at least they have survived the ordeal by statue. That's not too bad."

"Have they?" Lionel Twain snapped. "Have they, indeed? Look at that."

61

And, true enough, Milo Perrier had just made his way into the huge hall accompanied by the ever-faithful Marcel, feet first.

Puffing and plainly furious, Perrier was dragging his chauffeur's limp and unconscious body across the stone floor of the big room. At last on a small ledge under a particularly fearsome bunch of hanging weaponry he spotted a telephone. He let Marcel's feet drop.

"Didn't I say 'jump'?" he demanded of the recumbent body. " 'One, two three, jump,' I say. Why don't you listen to me?"

"Oh, leave me alone," Marcel, flat on his back, just succeeded in mumbling.

"Oh, yes," said the great detective, "leave you alone so that in future I have to buy my own ice creams."

"But you did buy your own ice cream," Marcel groaned. "That it why we were late arriving and that *diable* of a statue was falling on my head."

Up in the viewing room Benson smiled indulgently.

"You can always rely on Milo Perrier, sir," he said, "when it comes to a burst of mysterious action. To pretend to go and buy an ice cream so as to avoid that deadly trap. Very nice indeed, sir, I'm sure you'll agree."

"Imbecile," snarled Lionel Twain.

"Imbécile," Milo Perrier snarled down in the hall, glaring yet more fiercely at the still prostrate Marcel. "To try and embrace the Venus de Milo when you ought to know the lady has no arms. What response did you expect? Pah."

He turned to the phone and picked up the receiver.

"Allô?" he barked. *"Allô? Opérateur,* I am saying *Allô. Allô. Allô."*

"Dead, sir," pronounced a sepulchral voice from behind him. Benson had made use of the express lift.

Perrier whirled round, dropping the receiver.

"Who . . . who are you?" he asked.

"The butler, sir," replied Benson, resplendent in his full butler's uniform.

Perrier narrowed his eyes, which to tell the truth were rather piggy at the best of times.

"The butler, eh?" he said. "I thought as much."

"I am afraid the telephone is out of order, sir," Benson said loftily. "It has been so for the past week."

"Is that a fact?"

Perrier stooped and picked up the severed lead of the instrument. He examined it, eagle- and piggy-eyed. He smelled at the end.

"I put it to you," he said, holding the wire in front of Benson's sightless eyes, "that this wire has been snipped not one hour ago, as you can plainly see."

Silently Benson applauded. Little gray cells might be a bit old-fashioned, but they still got results.

"Now," Perrier went on, "since we cannot, it seems, call for a *docteur,* I will need a cold compress for my chauffeur and since my hair is a little deranged I would like a *coiffeur,* or at least a *miroir,* as well as a cup of hot chocolate, *n'est-ce pas?*"

"I don't think we have Nes-pas, sir," replied the imperturbable Benson. "However, we have all the usual brands. Hershey's, Cadbury's . . . I'll call the maid."

He crossed to the wall and after a long parade of searching at last encountered the bell cord. He pulled it vigorously three times.

In the kitchen Yetta, still sitting on her chair with her hands patiently folded on her lap, was staring into space waiting for orders. Lionel Twain's monitor camera caught her full face. He heard the bell on the wall buzz three times. Yetta sat just where she was, unblinking. The bell buzzed three times more. Yetta still sat. The bell buzzed again, once, twice, three times, loudly and angrily. Yetta blinked. Well, Twain thought, you have to blink sometimes.

Up in the hall Benson was frowning in anger.

"Oh, I'll fetch your chocolate myself, sir," he said pettishly. "In the meantime, if you'll be good enough to follow me to your room."

He turned toward the stairway. Perrier took a quick look at the recumbent Marcel, decided he was perfectly capable of walking on his own two feet, seized his arm, and dragged him sharply upright. The dazed chauffeur stumbled along in his master's wake.

"There is something about this butler I do not

63

trust," Perrier hissed to him. "Notice how he never looks directly at you."

"He is blind, *monsieur,*" the dazed but still reasonably registering Marcel answered.

"Nonsense," Perrier returned sharply.

He looked long and carefully at the butler tap-tapping his way in front of them up the huge staircase and sighing sadly under his breath.

But, as they marched down the length of the long, long corridor at the head of the stairs, the master detective evidently decided that it was time he showed who was the master. *Parbleu!*

He came hurrying up the tap-tap-tapping figure.

"I look forward to meeting our host," he said with heavy offhandedness, "although I think I can predict with some degree of accuracy that he stands no taller than five feet four inches."

He peered into Benson's face, looking for the expression of utter astonishment he is used in his books to seeing when he makes one of his truly amazing deductions. Benson's face remained blandly blank.

Perrier glared at him.

"Notice how low the paintings along here are hung?" he said furiously.

Still no reaction.

"Five feet four inches," Perrier shouted. "Am I correct?"

"He sounds small to me, sir," replied Benson, deferentially.

Perrier turned and gave Marcel a little wink. But Marcel was too busy thinking about his amorous encounter with half a ton of replica Venus de Milo to appreciate the full subtlety of his master's approach.

Perrier attacked the tap-tapping figure again.

"Just as I have noticed," he said, wagging his finger under the fellow's nose, "that you once served in your Majesty's Government in the North African campaign. Correct?"

Benson's eyebrows, above the dark glasses, rose a little at this.

"Yes, sir," he said. "But how—"

"Your erect posture has the bearing of a military

man," Perrier answered in triumph. "And you also step on the balls of your feet indicating years of walking on hot sand. Hah!"

"Amazing, sir," Benson said blandly. But he cast a distinctly triumphant look of his own in the direction, he hoped, of his master's camera.

He opened the door of the room chosen as specially suitable for the great Belgian detective and ushered Perrier and Marcel in.

"Dinner is at eight, sir," he said. "And I'll get the maid to bring you up your hot chocolate."

He bowed.

"One moment," Perrier snapped.

"Yes, sir?"

Perrier came striding up close to him and looked him squarely in the face. Then he puffed out his cheeks and stuck out his tongue.

Benson stood there stolidly, an expression of mild inquiry on his face.

Perrier put his thumbs to his ears and waggled his spread-out fingers.

Benson looked at him with the same expression of deferential interest.

Perrier violently rolled his eyeballs and contrived to move his scalp up and down as well as twitching his nose from right to left.

Benson inclined his head just a little, all ready to listen to any request made to him.

Perrier heaved a great sigh.

"Thank you," he said. "That will be all."

"Thank you, sir," said Benson gravely, turning and leaving them.

Perrier swung round to the still somewhat dazed Marcel.

"Those," he said portentously, "were my funniest faces. I tell you: that man is blind."

"Sir," Benson said, stepping out of the lift above, "they were really extremely funny faces. I had to think of my dear mother, sir, to prevent myself laughing."

7

Nothing that Benson could say, however, could put a stop to Lionel Twain's glee. He bounced out of his chair and hopped up and down the viewing room like a little rabbit.

"That little Belgian and his little gray cells," he said. "Pah, little gray sponges, more like. Why, he couldn't solve his way to the end of the alphabet."

"Monsieur Perrier has an immensely high reputation, sir," Benson said, "and besides I think his *moustaches* are charming."

"Charming, charming. The oldest gimmick in the book. A hero who's got nothing better to be ridiculously proud of than a pair of outsize mustaches. Kids' stuff."

"But, sir, there's his egg-shaped head."

"A fig for his egg-shaped head. And a fig for Sidney Wang and his Oriental aphorisms. And a fig for Dick and Dora Charlestons' wisecracks, too. I can do better myself any day."

"You have made a number of remarkable jokes, certainly, sir," Benson replied. "But may I remind you that there are still two sleuths who have yet to arrive?"

"All right," said Lionel Twain, jumping up momentarily onto the seat of his swivel chair. "All right, let 'em come. Let 'em come, and let's see how they make out. Help! Help! Help! Benson, get me down off this chair. I'm going to fall! I'm going to fall!"

Benson, with remarkable charity in the circumstances, held the chair still and helped his master down.

He received no thanks.

"Let 'em come," Lionel Twain repeated, as soon as both feet were firmly on the carpet. "Let 'em come. Where's Diamond? I want to see Diamond. And that broad, my God."

He snapped a couple of switches on the console.

"There's the place now," Sam Diamond was saying as a temporary rift in the fog allowed the headlights of the battered old T-bird to pick out the silhouette of No. 22 Lola Lane.

He turned to Tess, slumped in her wide seat in utter exhaustion beside him.

"You all right, angel?" he asked out of tight lips.

Tess groaned.

"My feet are killing me," she said. "Why didn't you tell me we needed oil before I went back for the gas?"

"Because I would have had to give you a fifty-dollar bill to pay for both, but I had change for the gas on its own," Sam answered. "And maybe you would have come back, maybe you wouldn't. I couldn't take that chance, angel."

"Don't you trust me, Sam?" Tess asked, her eyelashes fluttering hard.

"Trust you?"

Sam turned from the fog and looked straight into her eyes.

"Listen, baby, the last time I trusted a dame was in Paris in 1940. She said she was going to get a bottle of wine. Two hours later the Germans marched into France. I'll take my change now, sweetheart."

He held out his hand. Tess looked at him with sadness brimming out of her big, big eyes.

"Oh, sir, sir," said Benson. "Isn't he just fine? So tough, sir. So craggy. The most popular American in the whole of the British Isles, sir."

"Get up on that roof and start pushing that statue," Lionel Twain spat. "We'll see about tough. We'll see."

The T-bird came to a halt in front of the archway with the number 22 in large black figures above it.

Sam peered out, his mouth turned down.

"Not exactly Copacabana, is it?" he muttered through tight lips.

Tess gave a little shiver.

"I don't feel too good about this, Sam," she said. "Maybe tonight's the night when your luck runs out."

"Maybe so," Sam answered. "There's a number on the wall for all of us, angel, and if tonight's the night they pick mine, so be it."

Thank goodness, thought Lionel Twain, I sent Benson up to the roof.

Sam opened the car door and stood surveying the fog-wrapped pile. Tess came around to join him. He took her by the elbow and pushed her toward the tall, churchlike front door.

"After you, sweetheart."

She turned to him, tears brimming in her eyes. "First kiss me, Sam," she murmured.

Sam's face went hard.

"I don't kiss," he grated out.

Tess's eyelashes fluttered.

"Please, Sam, just this once."

Sam stamped his foot.

"I don't like kissing," he exclaimed furiously. "Leave me alone."

Above, Lionel Twain regretted sending Benson up to the roof.

Farther above, gloved hands pushed, pushed, pushed at the Statue of Liberty (reduced size), heaving, maneuvering and shunting all its half-ton weight slowly but inevitably toward the edge. Suddenly it sailed out into the darkness.

Benson turned, unable to bring himself to look down, and hurried for the lift and the kitchens.

There was the matter of his promise to Milo Perrier. A sleuth of his stature did not deserve to be kept waiting for hot chocolate, or for cold compresses. He seized a towel from a cupboard and held it under a stream of water at the sink. Then he busied himself preparing the chocolate.

In three minutes he was pouring it into a cup and setting cup and saucer neatly on a small tray. Just as he finished, a piercing terrified woman's scream rang and rang through the old house.

"Ah, the bell."

He turned to the newly arrived maid, whom he had not (how blind can a blind butler get?) seen sitting still on the chair she had occupied ever since she had been in the kitchen.

"Don't be frightened," he said. "That's just the bell. A little quirk of the master's. Will you answer it, please?"

Yetta paid no attention (how deaf can a deaf-and-dumb maid get?).

"Do you hear me?" Benson shouted.

Still no answer.

Benson gave a weary sigh.

"Never mind. I'll go. Here, you take this up to *Monsieur* Perrier, fourteenth room on the right in the west wing." He held the tray out to her. Deaf and dumb she might be, and also incapable of reading English, but when a tray was held out toward her it conveyed a message.

She took it. Benson hastily went to answer the front-door scream. Yetta looked at the tray. Well, a cold towel applied to the face is always refreshing. And a cup of hot chocolate is nice, too.

Upstairs, Benson crossed the length of the huge hall, his white cane before him, *tap, tap-tap, tap-tap-tap, tap,* arrived at last at the door, fumbled all over it flat-handed for the latch, located it eventually, and swung the big door back.

A girl was standing there. She was blond and all that needed to be said of her was that she had been around.

Benson heaved a sigh of relief. The Statue of Liberty had not proved too much for the sleuth from downtown.

Then beyond her, just in the frame of the doorway, he saw a pile of stone chunks from which there jutted —his heart gave a terrible thump—a pair of well-worn shoes such as might belong to a tough private eye with an office containing little more than a battered chair, a battered desk with a brass ashtray

70

always half-filled with butts and a layer of gray ash-flakes all over it twitching and crawling from time to time in the slow current of air coming through the half-opened window from the narrow court outside, faintly scented with ammonia.

Tess gave a sob.

"He . . . he's dead," she gulped.

But Benson knew the cameras were on him, whatever private grief he felt. "I beg your pardon," he said simply, putting into the words the full British aplomb.

"Sam Diamond," Tess jerked out between renewed sobs. "Sam Diamond, the man I work for. He's . . . he's lying out there. He . . . he's just been crushed to death."

She lurched forward half a pace till she was just inside the door.

"Oh, dear God," she murmured, "I'm going to faint. Catch me."

Benson was not an English-trained butler for nothing. He knew that when a visitor, and a lady visitor at that (well, almost a lady) asked to be caught, it was his duty to catch.

He extended his arms.

But Benson was not a blind butler for nothing. He extended his arms in the wrong direction.

Tess, eyes shut, body crumpling quite beautifully, landed with an almighty wallop on the hard stone floor.

"Madame, madame," exclaimed Benson, peering vaguely downward in the direction from which the almighty wallop had come. "Madame, are you quite well?"

"Awright, hold it."

The voice was American, tough American, the sort of voice that would belong to a private eye who had an office in downtown San Francisco which contained little more than a battered chair and a battered desk.

"Freeze, Dark Eyes," said Sam Diamond.

Happily Benson froze.

Sam pointed the forty-five he was holding in the direction of the blind butler's belly button.

"Get your hands up," he snarled. "And turn your face to the wall."

Benson managed the hands-up business fine. But the face-to-the-wall aspect presented a little more difficulty.

"In which direction, if you please, sir?" he inquired.

Sam seized him by the shoulders, twirled, and pushed. Benson discovered where the wall was.

"Like this, sir?"

"Like that, black eyes."

Sam turned his attention momentarily to Tess on the floor, reclining on her butt.

"All right, angel," he said, "you can get up now. Good work."

Tess pushed herself to her feet. She devoted some little attention to the butt.

"Yeah," Sam addressed the back of Benson's head. "I guess your concrete Christmas present arrived about two seconds too early, no thanks to you. Not very surprised when Miss Skeffington here told you I was lying out there dead as a clam, were you?"

He switched his gun from one hand to the other.

"Maybe," he went on, "the surprise is that I'm standing here breathing the same air as you. Isn't that right, 'my good man'?"

The irony was savage.

Oh, thought Benson, how exquisite. How admirably tough. How wrong I was to doubt him even for a moment.

"Look at that hand," Sam went on, though he did not seem to expect the butler actually to face around from the wall.

"Look at that hand. It's shaking. Well, I'm not usually that nervous. But that's how close you came to getting a forty-five slug right through your butler suit."

Benson's butler suit gave a top-to-bottom quiver of sheer appreciation.

"I apologize for any unfortunate mishap, sir," he said, as English as afternoon tea. "And may I put my hands down now?"

"Don't test your luck, Shakespeare," Sam fired

back. "I got your little invitation to dinner, only I didn't know I was gonna be the main course."

He switched the forty-five back to the other hand.

"Yeah," he said, "I had a kid brother who got it in the same way two years ago on a case just like this one. He would have been sixty-three on Thursday."

He shifted the gun around in his hand in a sudden wave of fury, ready to pistol-whip the butler-suited figure.

"For two cents I'd like to——"

"Sam! Don't!"

It was Tess.

Sam glowered at her. But his raised arm dropped.

"Get him away from me," he snarled. "Get him away before I stuff him like one of them tiger trophies."

Tess quickly took hold of the butler by the sleeve and led him off.

He gave a discreet little cough.

"He has a dreadful temper, hasn't he?" he said happily.

Back in the kitchen quarters, he reverted to more humdrum considerations. Thank goodness the extra help arrived all right, he thought, staring blindly around.

And the help was still sitting where she had been put, in the chair drawn up to the kitchen table. She had disposed of the nice cold towel which this strange man had been so kind as to offer and had drunk down her cup of hot chocolate (curious customs these foreigners have, but when in Rome do as the Romans do and when in America drink a cup of hot chocolate as soon as you arrive at a house).

"It's nearly eight o'clock," Benson said briskly. "Time for dinner."

The help, secure in her world of deaf-and-dumbness, looked at the strange man with mild interest (the customs of the natives are often a source of considerable intellectual speculation).

Getting no answer, Benson raised his voice.

"Nearly eight," he repeated. "Is everything ready?"

Then, with the still ongoing silence, something, some faint suspicion, began to grow in his mind.

Something was missing that ought to be there. In a kitchen just before dinner is served to ten guests there ought to be . . .

Ah, yes.

He lifted his head and gave a prolonged and savoring sniff.

"I don't smell anything," he said. "Very light on the seasoning, aren't you?"

The hired cook made no reply. Benson frowned.

"Put the soup in the tureen," he directed. "Keep the squabs on a low flame."

Yes, brilliantly deductive as ever, Milo Perrier had guessed right. Tender young pigeons, stewed to perfection in the most delicate of sauces, were on the menu for the dinner.

But only on the menu.

"I'll serve cocktails," Benson went on, ever resourceful. "When you hear the buzzer, turn up the flame under the squabs. Have you got that?"

No reply.

Well, Benson thought, some people are taciturn. Or uncommunicative. Or disinclined for idle chitchat. Put it how you like. It's the way they are. Live and let live, say I. If the girl doesn't want to talk, she doesn't. Let her just get on with the dinner preparations in her own fashion.

He made his way upstairs in the direction of the drawing room where cocktails were to be served before dinner.

Of course, back home in Britain where they know how things should be done, it would be sherry that would be served now, he thought. Sherry before a finely cooked dinner. But these Americans are barbarians, anyway, and they must be let have their barbarous customs. So cocktails it would be. Stirred, not shaken, served impeccably. A proper prelude to an excellent meal.

In the cold empty kitchen Yetta sat on.

8

Meanwhile the guests were preparing themselves to enjoy the civilized delights awaiting them. And the murder.

Dick and Dora Charleston had just finished dressing. They stepped out of their room. Dick in his dinner jacket with the rolled lapels (yes, rolled lapels) was the very figure of debonair perfection right to the last hair in his devilishly thin mustache. Dora matched him in elegance, in a very Thirties-style gown, brilliant in color and clinging where it ought to cling.

Outside their room a huge wall mirror in a heavy gilt frame glinted in the light from one of the few lamps in the dark and shadow-filled part of the house. Dora stopped in front of it and gave a little pirouette (no lady ever gives a big pirouette).

"You didn't tell me how I look, Dickie," she said, fishing like a tuna champion.

Dick came up behind her and inclined his head to her ear.

"You look no different than you always look, darling," he murmured. "Ravishing."

He planted a discreet kiss (not slobbery, discreet) on her bare shoulder.

A touching scene.

And a scene that had an observer. Behind the mirror was a big TV camera, and a sinister figure was drinking his fill of the touching little display of allurement and gallantry.

He watched Dora turn her head a little so as to look at Dick full in the eyes.

"Do you love and adore me?" she murmured.

Dick looked back full into her eyes and put a hand, a gentlemanly hand, on her bare shoulder.

"I love and adore you," he murmured back.

There was an edge of passion in his voice, clearly audible to the sinister watching figure.

In the deserted corridor Dick's hand slid slowly down Dora's shoulder. He gazed into her eyes. In his eyes a distinct hotness became visible. Up above a sinister figure drew in its breath. Sharply.

Dick's gentlemanly hand reached the small of Dora's back. His breathing became a trifle ungentlemanly around the edges. Dora looked hard into his eyes. On the receiving end of the gilt-framed mirror a sinister figure hopped into the air, once and briefly.

Dick's hand reached lower than the small of Dora's back. He leaned forward and spoke in a voice murmurous with ungentlemanly thoughts.

"Darling, you still have the best tush in high society."

Dora, hot-eyed in her turn, whispered back, "Years of horseback riding, darling."

On the far side of the mirror a sinister figure was hopping up and down, up and down. Rapidly.

A not-so-gentlemanly hand gave a horseback-improved tush a not-so-gentlemanly pat. (Tush! Tush!) Dora gave a great big shiver. A sinister figure started to slobber in a distinctly unsinister way.

But . . .

But farther along the shadow-filled and ill-lit corridor a bedroom door opened, casting a long bright stream of light out into the gloom. And silhouetted in that light stood a magnificent figure.

Dressed in a long, regal, marvelously colored and very ornamental full-length Chinese robe, together with a pair of equally ornamental Chinese slippers and on the head a little round ornamental Chinese cap, Sidney Wang was about to set forth for dinner.

Willie, dressed in an altogether not ornamental tuxedo, though managing like respected father to sport ornamental Chinese cap, followed him out into the corridor.

And nothing had escaped highly trained Chinese detective eyes.

"Ah, good evening, Charleston," Sidney Wang said with lots of impassivity. "Getting to the bottom of things?"

Dick and Dora wheeled around. There are some things you don't like to be seen doing in public. But Dick's sangfroid was equal to the occasion.

"Ah, Wang," he said, seeing who it was.

He turned to his wife.

"Dora, you remember—"

"Of course. So nice to see you, Ah Wang."

Sidney Wang gestured Son Number Three forward.

"Please to meet adopted son, Willie."

"Hi, there!" Willie said, seizing Dora's hand and vigorously shaking it.

Dora carefully ungummed her fingers.

All great friends together. On the surface. But underneath, each detective surely knew that the other was his sworn rival as World's Greatest Sleuth. And they were conscious, too, that it looked very much as if a definitive contest was about to take place for that honor. Why else would there be invitations to dinner . . . and a murder?

But the gathering of the contestants was by no means yet complete. Somewhere out in the fog a London taxi was still making its way toward No. 22 Lola Lane, its walrus-mustached old driver not in the least incommoded by this mere light mist but very conscious that there is a certain speed at which a London taxicab should go and that that speed is a crawl. And still only just sorting themselves out after a somewhat inauspicious arrival were Sam Diamond and Tess Skeffington.

Another door opened at that moment onto the ill-lit corridor and out of it emerged the celebrated Milo Perrier, closely followed by the uncelebrated Marcel.

Perrier was wearing a dinner suit of an extremely old-fashioned cut. Marcel was wearing a dinner suit, also of an extremely old-fashioned cut, plus a heavy pair of chauffeur's boots.

"Aha," Perrier said, spotting the group under the light that had made the big gold-framed mirror such an attraction. "Aha, so East meets West in a most—'ow you say—bizarre setting."

"Perrier!" Dick Charleston exclaimed. "I didn't know you were invited."

And underneath he thought, "So, it's to be a race with more than two runners, is it? Well, so much the better."

He gestured toward Sidney Wang.

"You know Wang?" he asked.

Perrier gave a stiffly formal bow.

"I had the pleasure of dining in Shanghai many years ago with Inspector Wang."

He drew in a quick little breath.

"Hong ching chu kow ding woo fong?" he asked, with all the nonchalance he could muster (and he was a pretty good musterer of nonchalance when the occasion arose).

Wang inclined his head.

"Yes," he said. "Very good. You remembered. You had *hong ching chu* and I had *kow ding woo fong.*"

Dick Charleston, ever mindful of the civilized decencies, performed more introductions.

"My wife, Dora . . . *Monsieur* Milo Perrier."

Perrier gave a low bow.

"Très charmante," he murmured.

Dora held out a lovely white hand.

Perrier bowed low again, bestowed on it the most elegant of kisses, and burst into an appalling fit of coughing.

"So sorry," Dora explained sweetly. "Our room is just a bit dusty somehow."

"My fault, Madame," Perrier replied, ever gallant. "I should have blown first."

He gestured toward the figure behind him in dinner suit and boots.

"May present my *secrétaire* and chauffeur, Marcel Cassette?"

Marcel gave a bow even lower, and hopefully more gallant, than his employer's.

78

"Recovered from your road accident, Marcel?" Dick Charleston asked at once.

Marcel looked at this stranger in surprise.

"*Oui, monsieur,*" he replied. "But how did you . . ."

Dick gave an easy wave of his hand.

"Oh, from the way you bend," he answered offhandedly. "The left side of your body smashed in by a Citroën, I imagine. I also detected a slight metallic sound which leads me to believe you had an artificial hip put in. Steel?"

"Aluminum," Milo Perrier replied, just managing to conceal his fury and chagrin. "You're as quick as ever, Charleston."

Dick gave a modest shrug. Modest shrugs were one of his specialties, practiced most mornings in front of a good-sized mirror, and he reckoned he had just about got the art taped.

Sidney Wang stepped forward, his impassive Oriental face wearing a more than usually impassive Oriental expression, a bit like a temple statue making strenuous efforts in a particularly high-stakes poker game.

"Hospital room number 403," he said. "Correct?"

Marcel was astonished. His jaw fell open. He gasped.

"*Mais oui,*" he said. "But . . . but how did you . . . ?"

Wang permitted the very faintest of smiles to curl about one quarter inch of the left-hand side of his top lip.

"Dr. Miguel Dos Passo only aluminum hip man in Europe," he explained. "His hospital is Our Lady of Pain in Madrid. Milo Perrier would want best for trusted servant, and best room in Our Lady of Pain Hospital in Madrid is number 403."

"Nice going, Pop," said young Willie, giving a cocky smile all around as much as to say, "Now you've seen what a really great detective can do."

"*Formidable,* Monsieur Wang," Milo Perrier said with a bow. "And may I say I regret very much that your dentist has died?"

Willie gaped.

"Holy cow!" he exclaimed. "How did you . . . ?"

"Mister Wang," Perrier explained, "has caps on two front teeth, one slightly whiter than the other. The

79

whiter one was done first and is clearly superior work. Why go to another dentist for an inferior cap? The answer is—'ow you say—obvious. The first dentist is either retired or dead. Since no superior dentist would retire in the middle of caps, he is most regrettably dead."

"*Touché* and double *touché,*" Marcel claimed enthusiastically.

But Sidney Wang was not done yet. He turned with a slight Chinese bow to Dick Charleston.

"And you, Mr. Charleston," he asked, "did not approve of Mrs. Charleston dying hair blond?"

Dick looked startled.

"I beg your pardon."

Wang permitted an even fainter smile to curl one-eighth of an inch of the left-hand side of his top lip.

"Mrs. Charleston's hair red," he explained. "You have blond hairs on shoulder, Mr. Charleston. That means Mrs. Charleston has dyed red hair blond, then back to red, or else you have been——"

He broke off. An expression of extreme social embarrassment appeared on his impassive Oriental face.

"Er . . . shall we go down to dinner, please?" he said.

Silently the party began to descend the huge staircase. Dora gave Dick a look that was about as angry as a nestful of hornets with sales tax added. Dick glanced up at the ceiling, down at the stairs under his feet, around at the walls, up at the ceiling again, down at the stairs under his feet once more. Anywhere but at Dora.

Just behind them, Willie Wang perked up his shoulders.

"Boy, Pop," he said, "you sure put your——"

"Shut Japanese mouth," came the swift parental injunction.

Still more than a little constrained, they continued their way down the big, picture-hung staircase to the promised cocktails, promised dinner, and promised murder. Milo Perrier and Sidney Wang, walking side by side, passed a large oil painting of a dog with lolling tongue looking piteously at an empty water bowl. (Very

80

touching, very heart-rending. Surely only a man of the greatest sensitivity and kindness could have such a picture on his walls.)

But as the pair of great detectives drew parallel with the painting a curious change came over it. The big brown faithful eyes of the dear pathetic little doggie abruptly disappeared. To be replaced by a pair of sharply glinting eyes looking distinctly human. The long lolling rough doggy tongue disappeared, too, and in its place came a human tongue, rather furred.

The two great detectives passed on their way. But behind them Willie Wang was in just the right position to notice the phenomenon.

"Hey, Pop.

The voice was raucous and loud.

But Sidney Wang had had much experience of ignoring that particular raucous and loud voice. He turned to Dick Charleston.

"Mista Charleston," he said, evidently recalling something he had been meaning to tell his colleague for some little time. "Mista Charleston, as I was pointing out to you earlier this evening, a treacherous road like fresh mushrooms. You must always—"

"Hey, Pop."

This time the loud and raucous voice was right in Sidney Wang's ear. Only a man with no eardrums could have ignored it. Sidney Wang came into this world complete with eardrums, and he had managed to retain these normal pieces of human equipment ever since.

He turned to his adopted son. His bland impassive Oriental face was contorted with unbland and by no means impassive universal rage.

"Why you not let me tell him about mushrooms?" he stormed.

Willie looked deeply offended at this adult injustice.

"But, Pop," he said. "But, Pop, the dog in the picture—"

"—has been watching us," Sidney Wang completed his son's sentence.

Willie gaped.

"You knew?"

"Noticed dog's eyes in picture," Wang replied, regaining all at once his Oriental impassivity. "Wearing contact lenses. Most unusual."

But Dora Charleston, who had overheard the exchange—as who wouldn't, given the loud raucousness of Willie's voice and the un-Oriental rage of his father at not getting over the point of his mushrooms and treacherous roads story yet once again—was very upset.

"Mr. Wang," she said, all fluttering, "you mean someone has been watching us?"

It was Milo Perrier, however, who undertook to answer, possibly feeling it was too long since he had impressively exercised his great detective's powers. He stepped forward.

"Someone has been watching us ever since we arrived, madame," he said. "I, Milo Perrier, have noticed it. Even the mirror up there near the head of the stairs has two sides—one for reflection, one for the—'ow you say?—the Peeping Tom."

Dora, her mind flashing back to a certain exchange of what you might call compliments, clutched . . .

Her tush.

Meanwhile out in the fog at last and at last a London taxicab had reached its destination.

"Ah," said Miss Jessica Marbles firmly from the back. "This must be it."

The final guest had arived. The party was complete. All was ready now for dinner. And a murder.

9

Lionel Twain shifted uneasily in his swivel chair. He glared at Benson.

"Is everything ready?" he asked with marked cantankerousness.

"Perfectly, sir," Benson replied.

He allowed his mind to play on what he had heard of the first meeting of the great detectives. There was no doubt that they had shown up to advantage, each and every one.

"What about Wang and his blond hair on the shoulder, eh?"

It was the voice of his master, interrupting a very pleasant strain of thought.

Benson drew himself up.

"One must expect a person of Mr. Charleston's charm to . . . er . . . play around, as I believe they say over here, sir," he said.

"And one must expect a so-called great detective to put his foot in it," Lionel Twain retorted.

"But how about the way he knew what hospital room Marcel Cassette had been in?" Benson snapped back.

"And how about his great deduction that Dick Charleston had been rather free with a certain tush?" Lionel Twain countered. "Very subtle detective work, that."

"I am unaware of the meaning of the word 'tush,'

sir," Benson replied, nose in air. "I can only suppose it to be American argot."

Lionel Twain glared at him.

"Well, it means—"

"I think, sir, I had better return to the kitchen. And I suspect that you had better keep an eye on your guests. One of them might outsmart you, sir, to employ an expression with which you must be familiar."

And, in a twinkling, Benson had gone. Lionel Twain sat for a few moments glaring at thin air. His expression hinted, too, at a trace of inner disquiet.

But almost at once he turned to his TV screens and selected channel 53—the drawing room.

All was awed silence in the room where cocktails were soon served. Awed silence because the room was designed to awe. It was a whole museum of horrors, tastefully arranged.

Fetishes from America, the rat-goddess from India, pretty little paintings of torture scenes, and the odd execution or two, sometimes with blood seeming to drip out of the painting and onto the frame and the wall below, half a dozen thumbscrews set out on the wall in a neat pattern, finger of birth-strangled babe, eye of newt and toe of frog, all preserved under glass with a charmingly carved frame around them—these and as many others made the room at once comfy and elegant.

Perhaps its chief ornament was over the broad mantelpiece. It was a death mark, the face twisted in excruciating agony and seeming almost to pulsate with hideousness.

Dick and Dora, in their silent parade of the ingenious and amusing things the room had to show, arrived at it last.

"He's a charming fellow," Dora said, breaking the long silence.

"African death mask," Dick said knowledgeably. "Died in some tribal ritual, I should think."

Milo Perrier came up behind them.

"I beg to differ," he interrupted, a cocky look plastered all over his egg-shaped face. "I have seen that expression before."

84

He wagged a solemn finger at them.

"This man," he said, "has died from a four-and-a-half-pound gallstone."

The Wangs and Marcel joined them in front of the malevolently crackling fire.

"Wonder where others are," Wang said with careful nonchalance.

"Others?" Dora asked. "What others?"

Wang looked at her solemnly.

"Invitation to dinner and murder finally clear to Wang," he said. "With appearance of Monsieur Perrier—"

But Milo Perrier himself jumped in to complete the thought.

"With the appearance of Milo Perrier himself," he said, "it becomes obvious that only the world's greatest living detectives are on the guest list."

Dick Charleston nodded agreement.

"Five of us to be exact, darling," he said to Dora. "Three are already here . . ."

"So," said Wang, "two have not arrived."

Perrier held up two fingers of his right hand (in a thoroughly delicate manner) and counted them off.

"One, Miss Jessie Marbles, of Sussex, England. And two, Mr.—"

The bursting open of the door interrupted him.

"Sam Diamond of San Francisco," came a voice through tight lips.

Sam was dressed in a white dinner jacket, double-breasted. Only a garment of that cut would easily conceal a forty-five worn in a shoulder holster. Beside and a little behind him was Tess in a strikingly colored flowsy gown. And a flowsy gown, in case you don't know, is a gown that suits a blowsy floozie.

Tight-lipped, Sam surveyed the assembled guests.

"I know who you all are," he said, making with the introductions. "And the lady here in the rented dress is my secretary and mistress, Miss Tess Skeffington."

"Aw, Sam," Tess said, "don't."

Sam gave her a careless look.

"Oh, I'm sorry, sweetheart," he said, as if it had only

85

just occurred to him that the description could possibly not be what she liked to hear.

He turned to his fellow investigators.

"Miss Skeffington doesn't like me to be so brutally honest," he explained. "But then again, we're all in a brutal business, aren't we, gentlemen?"

Sidney Wang looked offended, as far as an inscrutable Chinese could look anything.

"Never considered 'murder" to be a business, Mista Diamond," he said stiffly.

"Is that right?" Sam jerked back. "Well, maybe not for you, Mr. Wang, seeing as how you put all your money into vegetables back in the late Thirties."

He got a quick reaction in the inscrutable Chinese eyes and turned to the others with a glint of triumph.

"Maybe our friends here didn't know that you own over fifty percent of the bean sprouts and bamboo shoots grown on the Chinese mainland," he said. "So you folks can imagine how much chicken chow mein goes into Mr. Wang's pot every year."

He flicked around to Tess.

"Am I right, angel?" he asked, quick as a Thompson submachine gun.

"Right, Sam," Tess came back as fast.

Sam whirled again to Sidney Wang.

"You're good, Wang," he fast-talked. "You found a way to make crime pay. You can sashay here in your silk nightgown and your cute little pony tail hangin' down the back lookin' around for fingerprints through your squinty little eyes, but it's guys like me who have to do all the dirty work."

And he flicked around to Tess.

"Isn't that so, angel?"

"Right, Sam," Tess came back, faster than ever.

But now Milo Perrier entered the fray.

"I don't see what this——"

Sam cut across him like a shark slipping in front of a fat bather.

"Or you, Mr. Perrier," he said. "You've worked on both sides of the big drink. Pretty good pickings over there, solving crimes for them barons and earls and putting your fancy fees into private Swiss banks. Three

86

trips a year buys a lot of hot chocolate, doesn't it, Frenchie?"

He stepped back a little and favored the whole gathering with a wolfish leer.

"If I'm going too fast for you, folks," he said, "just let me know."

"See here, Diamond——" Dick Charleston began, quite ready to take him up on the "letting him know" line.

But Sam jumped in front of him as if he were a great hunk of traffic cop slapping to a halt the Charleston Rolls-Royce.

"No, you see here, Mr. Charleston of New York, Palm Beach, and Beverly Hills," he snapped. "Crime is just a hobby for you, isn't it? Just a little game to while away the time waiting for your room service in fancy hotels, while your wife's family dough pays for your gin martinis and your three-hundred-dollar suits."

He grinned like a predator as Dick Charleston's hands involuntarily went to the rolled lapels of his tuxedo.

"Yeah," he went on, the words still shouting out like bullets, "a pretty nice arrangement when all you gotta do is to give your wife a little grab every now and then and take the dog out for a leak twice a day."

He saw the look of offense on Dora's pretty face, and, come to that, on Tess Skeffington's not exactly pretty, but pretty sexy face, too. Because Tess, although she'd been around, knew how to put on a look of offense when she felt she was in the right company.

"Sorry if I'm shocking you, ladies," Sam went on. "But I never had time to go to finishing school. My school was the streets, and looking down the barrel of a pointed revolver was my teacher." He whirled back to his fellow sleuths and hammered on.

"I make fifty dollars a day and expenses, when I can get it, gentlemen." And I owe Miss Skeffington here three years and four months in back pay. Isn't that right, angel?"

But this time he did not get his "Right, Sam" fired back at him as quickly as he had fired his question at her. Instead Tess's big, big eyes went even big-bigger and she replied in a soulful, soulful voice.

"I don't care about the money, Sam."

"Neither do I." Sam came back faster than a striking rattlesnake.

He gave the assembled guests a long, beady look.

"I don't like you people any more than you like me," he told them. "Maybe dinner and a murder is an evening's pastime to a bunch of swells like you, but to a mug like me it's a crime to be solved and a shrimp cocktail."

He shrugged.

"I just thought I'd get things straight before the evening began."

His oration did not receive a round of hearty applause and cheering. Instead there was a long frozen silence.

Broken at last by Tess.

"Nice going, Sam," she said loyally.

Sam turned to her.

"I thought you'd like it, angel," he said.

He looked at the others again.

"And now," he said, "if one of you gentlemen will be so kind as to get my lady friend here a glass of cheap white wine, I'm gonna go out into the hall and look for the can. I talk so much sometimes I forget to go."

And, suiting the action to the word, he left, moving fast.

Keeping his knees together, too.

Mr. Twain's other guests looked at each other. Deep sighs could be heard floating up in all directions.

Tess heard most of them.

"Please excuse Sam," she said. "He was shot in the head last week. He shouldn't be out of the hospital."

Dick Charleston raised his eyebrows.

"Well, if you ask me," he said, looking around at them all, "the fellow's pretty damned honest."

"Dickie," said Dora. "Language."

Milo Perrier weighed in with his opinion on the departed whirlwind.

"He's no fool," he said thoughtfully. "That is for certain."

"Diamond may be rough," Sidney Wang added

wisely, "but he is great detective and dangerous one. I would not like to get on wrong side of him."

"Yes," Dick Charleston agreed. "He does spit when he talks, doesn't he?"

"Dickie," Dora warned him again. "Language."

But before further comments on Sam Diamond and his brutal honesty could be exchanged, the door to the drawing room was ceremoniously opened and blind old Benson presented himself.

"Miss Jessica Marbles," he announced. "And nurse."

From behind him came a curious couple. Seated in a wheelchair of magnificent antiquity, an affair of polished old mahogany, cane-backed, with plush-covered arms, iron-spoked wheels and the general air of being a machine from the early period of the Industrial Revolution, was an old, old woman, rug-hugging and shawl-wrapped. Pushing her was a lady of some fifteen summers less, a fairly hefty and spry septuagenarian, dressed in robust tweeds with good wool stockings bulging over sturdy calves and a face that was the epitome of all the no-nonsense expressions that have ever been expressed.

Sidney Wang was first to greet the illustrious sleuth from England.

He bowed deeply to the wheelchair.

"Miss Marbles," he said, "so we finally meet. Have admired you since I was tiny little detective."

He took the withered old hand of the beshawled and berugged figure and planted a tributary kiss upon it.

"Thank you, Mr. Wang," said—not the beshawled old lady, but the sturdy figure behind her.

Wang looked thoroughly disconcerted.

"I am Jessica Marbles," the lady pushing the chair announced sturdily. "This is Miss Withers, my nurse. She's been with me fifty-two years, and I have to take care of the poor dear now."

The aged, aged nurse nodded her aged, aged head. Miss Marbles stooped and bellowed into her ear.

"Are you all right, Miss Withers?"

The aged nurse nodded her aged head again as much as to say, "As well as can be expected at my age, which

89

is, as you may know, the late eighties. Yes, I said, late eighties. Remarkable, isn't it?"

Miss Marbles took a huge breath and bellowed again.

"Do you want your medicine now?"

The aged nurse nodded her aged head as much as to say, "No, I don't want my medicine, blast you. I've given too much medicine to too many disagreeable children in my time not to know that medicine's nasty stuff or it wouldn't be medicine. So is it likely that I would want my medicine? No, it is not."

"You take your nap now, dear," boomed Miss Marbles in her ear. "We'll be having din-din soon."

The aged nurse nodded again as much as to say, "Why do you have to speak to me as if I was a child? I'm a nurse, not a child. That's exactly the opposite thing. And, yes, now that you mention it, I could do with a bite too . . ."

But she had nodded herself to sleep. And a good thing, too.

Miss Marbles straightened her back and took a magisterial survey of the room, at once spotting a highly significant fact: that of those there assembled the majority had got drinks clutched in stout right hands.

"Hah," she said. "I could use a good stiff 'shot.' "

A fine old woman of the world, Miss Marbles. She knows her onions. All these Americans call a drink a shot. She's been to the pictures, down in Brighton it was, some time before the War. She knows what's what.

"Yes," she said, "A 'shot.' Mr. Charleston, I believe the 'booze,' as you people call it, is your department."

Dick Charleston raised his eyebrows. But only a fraction. He had a notion that if he raised them more he might get the sharp edge of this formidable old dear's tongue.

"My pleasure, madam," he said, heading for the side table on which there was a generous layout of all the drinks you could think of.

Sam Diamond came back in, his hands just leaving his trousers zipper. Jessie Marbles had her back to him. So, without preliminaries, he demanded of the room in general, "Who's this old geezer?"

Miss Marbles turned round.

It was a magnificent sight. Imagine (if you can) a battleship swiveling on its heel. Or, if that's a little difficult, imagine a battleship swiveling on its keel. That was the way Miss Marbles looked when she turned and surveyed the newcomer.

"The 'old geezer,' Mr. Diamond," she pronounced, "beat you at strip poker in Panama City seventeen years ago. Left you in cotton socks and your Fruit of the Looms."

Then Sam recognized her.

"Jessie! Baby!"

He stepped forward and gave her a great bear hug that lifted her, solid lady though she was, right off the ground.

"What are you doin' here, you crafty old bird?" he asked. "I thought nothing could ever get you out of that little hick Limey town of yours."

Miss Marbles drew herself up. And there was plenty to draw.

"Nothing, except pride, Sam," she answered. "The five greatest criminologists ever, assembled in one room. Someone is going to leave this house as Number One. And over somebody's dead body, that's going to be me."

Sam smiled.

"Feisty as ever," he said. "Give me a British broad every time."

And he landed her a happy slap on her excessively broad fanny.

"What room are you in?" Miss Marbles asked him.

"I'm with somebody," Sam answered at once.

What Jessie Marbles would have said history was not to record, if history would let itself record things like that in any case.

Suddenly the comparative peace of the big drawing room with its fantastic display of horror objects on the walls was rent—yes, rent—by a deathly moan.

"Quiet, please," called Sidney Wang with Chinese unnecessariness. "Observe strange sound."

But it was Dora Charleston who spotted just where the horrifying noise was issuing from.

91

"My God," she said, "it's the face. It's coming from the face."

With trembling finger she pointed at the *pièce de résistance* of the collection of horror objects around the walls of the gruesome room, the death mask over the fireplace.

Her husband strolled across and made a closer inspection.

"Yes," he said thoughtfully, "he's actually going through his final moments of death."

He turned to the others.

"What could it mean?" he asked.

No one had an answer.

Except a voice in the doorway.

They all wheeled.

It was Benson, eyes hidden behind his shades, white stick hanging loosely from his wrist, immaculate in his butler suit.

"It means dinner, sir," he answered Dick's question. "We don't possess a gong. Dinner is served."

Dinner.

Dinner is served.

When will the murder be served in its turn?

10

The dining room of the big old house was not furnished so gruesomely as the drawing room. There was not one single instrument of torture on view, unless you counted as a possibility the horns of a very large moose head hanging over the mantelpiece halfway down the long room. But this and an old-fashioned clock were the only ornaments. Otherwise severe oak paneling ran along all the walls, broken only on the side opposite the moose head by half a dozen tall windows, uncurtained so as to allow the rain to beat against them in a pleasant fashion, accompanied, as always in this house and thanks to the marvels of the electronic age, by plentiful zigzag flashes of lightning and many a roll and crack of thunder. All down the middle of the long room ran a wide dining table, and at this were sitting the five sleuths and their five companions.

They were under observation, needless to say.

"Yes, Benson," Lionel Twain remarked, briskly rubbing the palms of his hands together. "I think we can say that Dora Charleston is well and truly on the run. She can hardly open her mouth now without giving a gasp of horror."

"It would seem so, sir. Poor lady."

"Poor lady, poor lady. She's meant to be a little firework of a wisecracker, isn't she? Well, she certainly isn't living up to the book."

"Nevertheless, sir, she is still delightfully in love with Mr. Charleston."

"Except when she thinks of that blond hair your Chinese super-sleuth opened his gabby mouth about."

"An unfortunate episode, sir, no more."

"Unfortunate, yes. Episode, oh no. Just merely typical of your heroes, Benson. Just one more piece of typical ineptitude."

Benson looked pained.

He made no remark out loud. But a number of thoughts went through his mind. Like, Miss Marbles has only just come and she seems to be in splendid form. And how about Sam Diamond? You couldn't wish for tougher talk than we've had from him so far.

"And as for Sam Diamond," said his employer, cunningly breaking into the silence, "there have been one or two significant remarks there already. I have great hopes for Sam Diamond."

"So have I, sir," Benson said, forcefully as a good butler could. "And now, if you'll excuse me, sir, I have my duties."

"By all means, Benson. You have your duties, and I have my pleasures. And I bet I'm going to see plenty of those in the next few minutes. While you, let me tell you, are going to have rather heavier duties, old man, than you bargained for."

But Benson had left before the last warning words, and Lionel Twain turned happily to survey the long dining table with its ten places elaborately set with silver and glasses and at its head an empty chair. So far the guests had not gotten as much as a bite to eat, although earlier the blind butler had at least poured each one of them a glass of wine.

Dick Charleston was just rising to his feet with his glass in his hand.

"Ladies and gentlemen," he said.

A sudden hush fell.

"Ladies and gentlemen, I should like to propose a toast."

Nine pairs of eyes looked at him with interest. No, ten pairs. Where was the tenth? Had the host suddenly appeared? He had not. The tenth pair of eyes belonged to the moose hanging above the big stone mantelpiece. But, though they were in the place where a moose's eyes ought to be (which is on either side of a moose's nose) they did not look like a moose's eyes, which are soft, brown, and rather beautiful. They looked like a human's eyes, which are sharp, a whole range of colors, and generally pretty mean.

"Our host," Dick Charleston went on when he had caught everybody's attention, "our host, Mr. Lionel Twain, is indeed a most unique man."

He paused to let that sink in, bad grammar and all.

"Point One," he went on, "he has succeeded in gathering the world's five greatest detectives to investigate a crime that has not yet been committed."

He let that sink in.

"Point Two. He has set traps for us. A bridge that almost collapsed. Falling statues . . . Does he mean to kill us?"

He paused again. No one around the table was unfair enough to offer an answer and spoil his speech.

Dick supplied the answer.

"Does he mean to kill us? Certainly not yet. He could have done that at any time. He is merely trying to whet our appetites for the game that is to follow."

Again he paused.

"Point Three," he resumed. "Why five detectives, and not one? Because he means to take us all on, ladies and gentlemen, a feat no criminal mind has heretofore attempted."

Again he halted. Here was something that needed quite a while to sink in. The enormity of it, the sheer enormity.

"So," he said at last. "So, I propose, before this hellish evening begins, that we raise our wineglasses in toast to either a most beguiling and charming man . . ."

He let that thought hover in the air a while.

". . . or to an insidious, fiendish madman. Bottoms up."

They rose as one, lifted their glasses high, put them to their lips.

"One moment, please!"

The words, rapped out in a tone of fierce command, were from Sidney Wang.

They lowered their glasses and looked at him.

"Point Four," he said with Oriental blandness. "Wine is poisoned."

They gasped as one man, or woman.

"What—" exclaimed Willie Wang.

"Good heavens!" Dora gasped once again (much to the pleasure of Lionel Twain).

Sidney Wang sniffed at the contents of his glass.

"An ancient, odorless, colorless, and tasteless Oriental herb," he pronounced, "one that kills instantly."

He tipped the glass so that the wine in it poured in a steady stream onto the immaculate white tablecloth. A little column of blackish smoke rose up, and a small hole was burned in the cloth.

"Great Scot, Mr. Wang!" Dora said, even more gaspingly. "You saved our lives."

In his hiding place Lionel Twain gave a long chuckle.

"Not quite, Mrs. Charleston," Milo Perrier put in from his end of the table.

Lionel Twain's chuckle came to an abrupt halt.

Milo Perrier picked up his glass again, gave it a brief, appraising wine-lover's sniff, and then took a healthy swig.

Great big gasp all around the table. Milo Perier smiled with ill-concealed triumph and calmly finished off the glass.

"Since Mr. Wang here," he explained, "is the only one among us who has the ability to detect an Oriental poison of that sort, he was the only one who was tested."

He flashed them all a bright smile from under his twirling mustaches.

"Point Five," he added. "Mr. Twain is both beguiling and fiendish."

But suddenly onto his egg-shaped face there came a look of acute physical pain. His convulsed hands clutched at his stomach. His face went as white as if he were the victim of ungovernable anger.

Dora, who had been craning forward to watch him, leaped to her feet.

"Quick," she cried, "get a doctor."

"No, no," moaned Milo Perrier, still clutching his

stomach. "No, it's all right. My wine is not poisoned. It was just a very bad year."

From the other end of the table Sam Diamond leaned forward.

"You're all forgetting one thing," he said, out of tight lips. "This makes that butler pretty suspicious, since he was the one who poured the drinks."

But Milo Perrier was not impressed.

"The butler, *oui*. Except, *monsieur,* for the fact that he is blind. How would he know which one to serve the poison glass to?"

"That's simple enough," Sam retorted, out of tight lips. "Blind people have a very keen sense of smell. Since we are all Anglo-Saxon and Mr. Wang's son is Japanese, it wouldn't be very hard to sniff out the Chinaman."

Dick Charleston looked pained.

"See here, Diamond," he said, very stiff indeed. "That's a pretty tacky thing to say, isn't it?"

"It's a tacky world, Mr. Charleston," Sam hit back. "Isn't that right, angel?"

From Tess's place on the other side of the table came the quick answer.

"Right, Sam."

"Quiet, please," Sidney Wang broke in. "Butler approaches."

All eyes turned to the entrance archway at the other end of the long table from the empty chair. Benson entered carrying a large soup tureen, balanced on the outspread palm of his left hand. In his right hand his white cane felt out the way for him.

"I am sorry for the slight delay, ladies and gentlemen," he announced. "I seem to be having some communication trouble with our cook."

He tap-tapped his way to Miss Marble's place, slipped the cane onto his wrist by its strap, took off the cover of the big tureen, and stirred the contents with the ladle jutting out from it.

"Who poured the wine, Dark Eyes?" Sam Diamond demanded.

"Sir?"

"I said, who poured the wine?"

97

"Mr. Twain did, sir," Benson answered, smooth as oil. "It was left for me on a tray in the refrigerator. I was told to give Mr. Wang the glass with the sticky stem."

There was a short silence. Dick Charleston broke it.

"And you didn't bother to ask why?"

"I was lucky to find the refrigerator, sir," Benson answered.

He coughed discreetly.

"If I may serve the soup now?"

He moved around to Dora's place and with equal dexterity and generosity ladled her two large spoonfuls of nothing.

Perrier looked at him in astonishment.

"Just a moment, my man," he said, "where is the soup?"

"In the lady's bowl, sir."

"There is nothing in her bowl but her bowl," Perrier said.

"I'm afraid I do not understand, sir."

Perrier jumped up and went around to where the butler was standing, took the ladle, and held it up to his lips.

"Here. Taste it for yourself."

Benson tasted.

"I see what you mean, sir," he said, after judiciously smacking his lips. "If you'll excuse me, I had better have a little talk with the cook."

Still bearing the tureen in his left hand he made his way out. *Tap-tap, tap-tap. Tap. Tap-tap-tap.*

"Murder by starvation," said Miss Marbles thoughtfully. "Maybe that's his game, eh? What do you think, Sam?"

"I don't know, Jess," Sam answered, out of tight lips. "Why don't you ask that moose on the wall? He's been watching us since we came in."

Every glance focused in an instant on the moose. Its eyes hastily closed.

Meanwhile, back in the kitchen, Benson, who had failed to get any sense out of the maid, still sitting tranquilly in her chair at the big table, was furiously rummaging through the closets, his fingers feeling their

98

way over a maze of tin cans like ten little white sausages joining in a dance.

"All these people invited to dinner," he muttered. "And what are we serving? Hot nothing."

He turned to glare, sightlessly, in the direction of his co-worker.

"You're dismissed," he barked. "Fired. That's what they say in this country. You're fired, do you understand?"

Sitting tranquilly in her chair, deaf-and-dumb Yetta looked with mild interest at this foreigner.

He glared at her with redoubled fury, or at any rate more or less at her.

"I want you out, do you hear?" he stormed.

He crossed to the back door and after a little fumbling around, found it and flung it wide.

"OUT!" he yelled.

Yetta sat facing front at the table.

Benson stood by the wide-open door till he judged the girl must have got well through it.

"And stay out," he yelled into the foggy night.

Meanwhile, up in the dining room polite conversation was going on in the absence of any soup (*slurp, slurp*) or any wine reasonably safe from the chance of being poisoned (*sip, spit*). Gay laughter abounded.

Sam Diamond and Miss Marbles were exchanging a quip or two. Dick Charleston and Dora were trying to get the question of the Moores of Scotland and their move to Kent straightened out once and for all. Sidney Wang had begun to tell Willie about mushrooms and treacherous roads as a sort of warm-up before giving the definitive version to Dick. Milo Perrier was proposing to his *secrétaire*-cum-chauffeur an expedition to the kitchen to see whether a cup of hot chocolate couldn't be rustled up. Tess was telling Nurse Withers a few facts of life. Nurse Withers was dozing happily. When suddenly . . . Bang.

Out went the lights. Every last one.

The room was plunged into (guess what?) total darkness.

"Don't panic," Sidney Wang called out, in an imperturbably Chinese and plainly panic-stricken manner. "No one move from place, please."

"Someone just came into the room," Dick's voice came in the darkness. "I hear footsteps."

"Wait!" Milo Perrier commanded. "Quiet, everyone . . . I smell something."

"What is it?" Miss Marbles asked the pitchy black.

Perrier could be heard delicately sniffing. At last he spoke.

"Good God!" he exclaimed.

"What . . . what is it?" Dora asked gaspingly.

Perrier's voice in the darkness was charged with horror.

"It is franks and beans."

"I'm afraid, sir," came Benson's plummy tones, "that that is all we have."

General gloom. And then from the blackness there came the sudden sound, the appalling sound, of a high-pitched, nerve-racking electronic wail.

Nerves were racked.

But worse was to follow.

The darkness began to give way. Around the area of the empty host's chair a sort of light began to form. It was shimmering. No doubt about it, shimmering.

But then worse lay ahead.

From the shimmering light came a voice.

"Good evening, ladies and gentlemen," it said. "I am your host."

11

Every person in the still dark dining room recognized instantly that the voice which had just announced itself as belonging to their host was Truman Capote-like. Not that Nurse Withers had ever heard of the celebrated author of *Selected Writings* (1963), but she was not going to let the side down. Not for nothing had she played cricket for Sussex in that marvelous season of 1911. She would play her part now, the game old stick.

And then in the still shimmering light the voice spoke again.

"Yes, ladies and gentlemen, I am your host, Lionel Twain."

The shimmering light shimmered itself into an array of colors. And, not content with that, it shimmered itself next into nothing less than a silhouette.

It could do no more. Gradually the lights came up all over the room and the shimmer was no longer visible. Instead, the silhouette was revealed as that of a small man aged about forty, wearing a pink tuxedo, smoking a cigarette in a long holder, with colored spectacles across the bridge of his nose and a white Panama hat on his head. He looked, as everyone present including Nurse Withers instantly recognized, very like Truman Capote, celebrated author of *Selected Writings* (1963).

"Good God," said Jessie Marbles, "what an entrance."

101

The Truman Capote-like guy smiled with modest diffidence.

"A bit theatrical, Miss Marbles," he said, "but I do so love illusion."

His hand went to the brim of his Panama.

"Please forgive the hat, but I'm losing my hair."

Sam Diamond looked at him suspiciously.

"I thought Twain was an older man," he said. "Say seventy-two, seventy-three."

"Seventy-six to be exact, Mr. Diamond," the pink-tuxedoed figure came sharply back. "How do I look so young? Quite simple. A complete vegetable diet, twelve hours sleep a night, and lots and lots of makeup."

He looked around the faces at the table.

"I trust you've all been made comfortable," he added, with the hint of a sly smile.

"Comfortable?" Dick Charleston replied. "Do you call poisoned wine and near obliteration under falling statues 'comfortable,' Mr. Twain?"

"No," Twain admitted. "I call it 'inspiration.' The inspiration of a highly fertile and complex brain. *Ding chow soo ling tow,* as they say in Mandarin Chinese. Correct, Mr. Wang?"

"Afraid I do not speak Mandarin," Wang replied. "Just plain Chinese."

"I speak Mandarin," Miss Marbles claimed at once. She turned to her fellow guests.

"He said: a highly fertile and complex brain."

"He already said it in English," growled Sam Diamond. "What's the little squirt wastin' our time sayin' it in Mandarin for?"

He turned to Benson.

"Hey, Dark Eyes, how about a shot of bourbon?"

"Bourbon, sir," replied Benson, all British butler. "Yes, sir."

But Dora was not so immune to insult.

"Mr. Diamond, that's bad taste."

"Really?" said Sam inquiringly. "I like bourbon."

But now it was Milo Perrier's turn. He pointed a finger at their host and his twin mustaches quivered with suppressed fury.

"You have still not explained the various mechanical

and culinary attempts on our lives, *Monsieur* Twain," he accused.

Twain smiled.

"Merely games, *Monsieur* Perrier. Pitting wits with you, so to speak, to prepare for the big game still to come."

"You pit your wits with me," Sam Diamond retorted, jumping to his feet, "and you soon won't have any wits to pit with. Know what I mean?"

The forceful language woke Nurse Withers. She raised an ancient hand to her face and wiped it with her napkin.

"Sam," Tess whispered, in a voice that reached every corner of the table. "You're spitting on the nurse."

"Sorry, old lady," Sam said out of tight lips.

He turned to Milo Perrier opposite him.

"Crazy broad should be in bed," he said.

"Mr. Twain," Perrier said firmly, "we have been here nearly four hours, and there has not been a hint of a hot dinner. Nor a cold corpse."

He sighed theatrically.

"I am a busy man, Monsieur Twain," he continued. "I have other—'ow you say—Dover sole to fry. If you have nothing more to offer us but a few amateur theatricalities, I must bid you adieu."

He got to his feet, theatrically. And hauled chauffeur-cum-*secrétaire* Marcel up to his feet, equally theatrically.

Miss Marbles also rose.

"I'll bid one adieu as well," she said, wisely refraining from attempting to haul Nurse Withers to her feet. "Could someone call me a taxi, an English taxi, if you please?"

But, if Nurse Withers had not been hauled to her feet, she had at least been wakened from her renewed zizz.

She looked up plaintively.

"No murder-poo?" she asked.

"No, dear," said Miss Marbles soothingly. "Perhaps we can find a little something on the boat."

She reached down and picked up her purse.

But Lionel Twain spoke sharply before she could take even one step away from the table.

"I'm sorry if I appear an ungracious host," he said. "But no one is to leave this house."

He stooped and pressed a little button on a small panel on the under edge of the table. Instantly shutters on the tall windows clanged shut and from above and below automatic bolts clicked into place.

In the huge entrance hall, with its cluster of weapons, silent ominous suits of armor and broken-wire telephone, bolts whammed into place across the big front door. Even in the kitchen, where Yetta the maid was still sitting tranquilly, bolts sealed off the back door. At every window in all the house shutters clanged.

"Try the windows and the doors if you wish, ladies and gentlemen," Twain said. "But we are sealed in, I promise you. Like it or not, you are my guests."

"Well, I don't like it, you minty little Barbie Doll," growled Sam Diamond. "Open them doors, before I use your head for a key."

But Twain only shrugged politely.

"I'm afraid I can't, Mr. Diamond," he said. "We're on a time lock. Neither heaven nor hell can get in or out of this house before dawn tomorrow. We are here, trapped."

"Good God, Dickie," Dora said, her voice betraying a thousand unknown fears. "How will we take Myron for a walk?"

But Sidney Wang had a question more to the purpose.

"What is meaning of this, Mista Twain?"

"I will tell you, Mr. Wang," Twain replied, beginning to look a little edgy. "I will tell you if you will first explain to me why a man like yourself, who possesses one of the most brilliant minds of the century, cannot say prepositions or articles. *The,* Mr. Wang. You should have said: What is *the* meaning of this?"

"Very clever of you to notice, Mista Twain," replied the Chinese detective. "In solving crime, time is of essence. Prepositions take too much essence. Last year did not say thirty-two thousand prepositions, solved twenty-six murders. Point made?"

"Point made, Mr. Wang," Twain conceded sulkily.

"Now," Wang repeated cheerfully, "what is meaning of this, Mr. Twain?"

"The meaning of this, ladies and gentlemen," Twain answered, regaining his lost authority, "is that I have set out to prove beyond the shadow of a doubt that the greatest single living criminologist in the world is sitting at this table—and you are all looking at him."

They all turned and looked at each other. A spasm of annoyance passed over the baby-pink face of their host.

"Don't look at each other," he shouted. "Look at me! I'm the best. Me, me, me. I'm Number One. Do you understand? I—am—Number—One!!!"

"To me," Sam Diamond said, out of tight lips, "you look like Number Two. Know what I mena?"

"What does he mean, Miss Skeffington?" Dora whispered. .

"I'll tell you later," Tess whispered back. "It's disgusting."

"In all of your various adventures, ladies and gentlemen," Twain said firmly, sensing some whispering among his audience, "not one of you has ever had an unsolved murder. Your reputations exist on this single fact. But what would the world say if the five greatest detectives were trapped in a country house, completely cut off from the outside, only to discover a dead body on the floor, stabbed in the back twelve times with a butcher's knife . . . and not one of you was able to solve the crime?"

"You mean 'murder'?" Dora asked breathlessly.

"Please, Dora," her husband rebuked her, "we're talking shop."

"Yes, Mrs. Charleston," Twain answered sharply. "Murder. On the stroke of midnight, someone in this house will be viciously murdered, stabbed in the back eleven times with a butcher's knife."

"You said twelve times," Miss Marbles objected, with ruthless logic.

"Eleven, twelve, what's the difference," Twain snapped back. "What's the difference, as long as it's murder?"

He had given them all something to think about, and

a silence descended temporarily around the long table.

It was broken by Sidney Wang.

"Left out one small detail," he said. "Who victim?"

Rage flooded that pretty pink face.

"Is *the*," Twain yelled in uncontrolled fury. "Is *the*. Is *the*. Who is *the* victim? That nonsense of yours is driving me crazy."

"Sounds like a short ride to me," Sam Diamond said, out of tight lips.

"Does it, Mr. Diamond?" Twain yelled back, his eyes bulging. "Well, we'll see who's the crazy one and who's sane. The victim, Mr. Wang, is sitting at this very table at this very moment."

He glared around at them all in triumph.

"And so," he added, his voice rising to a shriek of glee, "is the murderer."

And the gleeful shriek had its effect.

Nurse Withers raised her head from her snooze.

"Murder-poo?" she asked.

"Yes, dear," Miss Marbles said solemnly. "We're going to have a lovely murder-poo."

Sam Diamond gave the ancient lady in the wheelchair a hard-nosed glare.

"Whyn't you push her down the driveway," he said to Jessie Marbles. "We got business here."

He turned to Twain.

"You say you know who's gonna get it?"

"Intimately," replied Twain with a wicked little giggle.

Milo Perrier jumped in.

"And you know how the crime is to be committed?" he asked.

"Definitely," said Twain with another little giggle.

"And exactly what time murder is to take place?" Sidney Wang joined the chorus.

"*The* murder," Twain corrected him. "*The* murder time. Precisely."

"Well," Dora chipped in, "it's none of my business, but doesn't that mean that you're the murderer, Mr. Twain?"

Twain looked sharply and huffily in the opposite direction.

"No wives," he said. "I will not discuss this with wives."

"*The* wives," Wang rounded on him in high Oriental triumph.

Twain swung around in redoubled fury.

"Not in this case," he yelled. "Not in this case. I meant the generic use of wives."

"Crazy language," Wang said.

Dick Charleston brought the temperature down.

"But Dora's quite right, old boy," he said easily. "All the fingers do seem to point to you. Not much of a challenge, I'd say."

Twain smiled.

"Shall I make it more interesting, Mr. Charleston?" he taunted. "One million dollars to the one who solves the crime. One million dollars wagered against your reputation. One million tax-free cash dollars, delivered in an envelope when the murderer is revealed."

Still he did not seem quite to have tempted them. He added one more inducement.

"In addition," he crooned, his voice tempting as the devil's, "in addition, all paperback rights and the film sale."

"Foreign and domestic?" snapped Jessie Marbles, quick as a striking rattlesnake, and speaking for them all.

"And I still get my fifty bucks a day?" added Sam Diamond.

For answer Lionel Twain slipped out his pocket watch and examined its dial.

"Eleven o'clock," he announced. "You have one hour, ladies and gentlemen. One hour until death strikes someone in this room."

The faces around the long table reflected the impact of his challenge. Miss Marbles was grim and thoughtful. Dick Charleston, though outwardly calm and debonair, had a cold sparkle in his eyes. Dora, looking at him, seemed simultaneously both stimulated and apprehensive. Next to her, Sidney Wang was impassively Oriental, but with a tiny crease of thoughtfulness on his forehead that betrayed the rapid working of the brain within. Tess Skeffington, in the next place, looked

107

anxiously across the table at Sam. Marcel, next to her, turned and regarded his boss with a look of doglike trust. And Perrier could be seen visibly puffing himself up at the thought of a contest which he could not doubt he would win. Sam Diamond, plainly, was thinking, out of tight lips, that this was a tough deal and that a tough guy was needed to set it to rights. Next to him Willie Wang was looking just plain excited. And next to Willie, Nurse Withers was . . .

Asleep.

"We got an hour?" said Sam, looking at the snoring old creature. "If you ask me, this one's only got about fifteen minutes."

At the head of the table Lionel Twain gave a little malice-full smile.

"I suggest you all retire to your rooms," he said, "and lock your doors from the inside."

His smile became broader.

"Not that it's going to help a certain someone at this table," he added with a little trickle of giggling.

Tess swallowed hard.

"I only work nine to five," she said. "Can I go home, please?"

Sam leaped to her defense, glaring at Twain and speaking out of tight lips.

"She's right, skinhead. Your quarrel is with us detectives. Why don't you let the others go and keep the five dicks here?"

Dora shot him an angry glance.

"Don't look at me," he snapped. "You're the one with the dirty mind."

From his chair at the table head Twain replied coolly.

"It's too late, Mr. Diamond. We're all in it now. For keepsies. See you at midnight."

He giggled with renewed malice, leaned forward, pressed another button on the panel under the table, and suddenly the whole big room was plunged into darkness again.

A woman's scream rang and rang through the impenetrable blackness.

108

"Stop that screaming," Sidney Wang shouted in a voice of sharp command.

"Sorry, Pop," said a chastened Willie. "Won't do it again."

As suddenly as they had been extinguished, all the lights flooded on again.

'See here, *Monsieur* Twain," Milo Perrier said angrily.

But there was no one in the host's chair.

"He's gone," said Miss Marbles. "Gone."

"No, he ain't," Sam Diamond's voice came unexpectedly. "He's here."

They all turned. And there at the far end of the table, sitting smiling like a grinning pink toad, was their host.

"Fast little bunny rabbit, ain't you?" Sam said.

"I've never moved, Mr. Diamond," Lionel Twain assured him. "A clever device employing a number of mirrors, that's all."

He smiled.

"Actually," he added, "I'm not even sitting here at this moment."

"Is that so?" Sam challenged him, pulling his forty-five from his shoulder holster. "You willing to risk seven years of bad luck?"

But Twain smiled again.

"Try it, Mr. Diamond," he jeered.

"It's your funeral, Butterball," Sam said.

He raised the gun and aimed it dead center at the button of that pink tuxedo. Then he slowly moved his aim upward.

"Let's see if you can catch a bullet between your teeth," he said.

"WAIT!" Twain shouted in a sudden agony of apprehension.

He smiled a little palely and explained.

"It . . . er . . . doesn't always work."

A look of sardonic triumph came over Sam's face, and he slowly put the forty-five back in its holster under the white dinner jacket. He turned and gave the others a heavy wink.

"You won that round, Mr. Diamond," said Twain,

rather snappishly. "But my turn comes at midnight."

He pressed a button on the arm of his chair. The whole chair zoomed backwards with him in it. Doors in the oak paneling behind him whirred noiselessly open. They swallowed him up, whirred noisily closed (installers are so bad nowadays), and it was as if he had never been there.

"Well," Sam Diamond said slowly, and out of tight lips, "if you ask me, anybody that offers a million bucks to solve a crime that ain't been committed yet has lost a lot more upstairs than his hair."

He turned to Tess.

"Ain't that right, angel?"

But Tess had been too scared by events to be her usual self.

"Oh, shut up, already," she snapped back.

Sam looked profoundly hurt.

"Well," Dora said brightly, ever the one to fill an awkward gap in the conversation, "what do we do now, just wait around to be butchered?"

Nurse Withers perked up at that.

"Butcher-poo?" she asked.

"Not yet, dear," Miss Marbles yelled reassuringly in her ear. "We have another hour to go. I'll let you know when."

Nurse Withers happily resumed her little snooze.

"And what," asked Milo Perrier dramatically, "has happened to the butler? Why has he not returned with our dinner?"

He tapped Marcel sharply on the head.

"Go and look for him."

"*Oui, monsieur.*"

"No!"

It was Sidney Wang, his old Oriental tone of command at full pitch. Marcel stopped in his tracks like an electric train in a power cut.

"No one is to leave this room," Wang ordered.

"Why not, Pop?" Willie asked innocently (what would a detective do without someone to ask innocently?)

"Mr. Twain say somebody at this table is victim,"

Wang answered. "If all stay together, crime cannot be committed without witnesses."

"He's right," Sam Diamond conceded. "You're one smart Chinaman, Mr. Wang."

"I suggest," said Jessie Marbles, "that we all join hands. The chain is stronger if the links are unbroken."

They reached out to each other's hands.

"What fun," said Dora with a little squeak of pleasure.

Miss Marbles straightened her shoulders under her thick tweed jacket and looked at her.

"Murder is not fun, Mrs. Charleston," she pronounced. "It may be entertaining, but it is never fun."

12

The big clock in the dining room of the locked, barred, and bolted house, with its oppressive ticktocking sound and its grim old-fashioned Roman numerals, had solemnly counted out twenty-two minutes since Lionel Twain had made his dramatic announcement and dramatic disappearance at precisely eleven o'clock.

Suddenly Sam Diamond, who in the general reshuffle that had followed Lionel Twain's departure and their all sitting down again had ended up next to the snoozing form of Nurse Withers, broke the tense silence of the big room.

"Stop that!"

Everyone jumped. But they kept holding hands and no one dared say a word.

Tick, went the old clock, time's passing. *Tock,* stop fussing. Silence descended again.

Only, within about half a minute, to be broken once more by Sam speaking loudly out of tight lips.

"Stop it, I said."

This time curiosity overcame discretion.

"What is it, Diamond?" Dick Charleston asked.

"The nurse is giving my palm the finger," Sam answered. "That dirty old broad."

"Naughty, naughty, Miss Withers," Jessie Marbles rebuked her.

Miss Withers giggled, a tiny little giggle like a leaking little tap.

113

But the minuscule sound was suddenly and sharply overwhelmed.

"Good God!"

It was Dora Charleston, her voice taut with choked fear.

"What is it?" Milo Pierrier asked, for them all.

"Look!" said Dora.

She wrenched one hand free and pointed toward the door.

There in the doorway stood the deaf-and-dumb cook. Her face was ashen white, her mouth was wide, wide open, her lips straining. Her whole body was stiff with effort.

"What—" said Tess Skeffington in a terrified whisper. "What is she doing?"

"I think," Miss Marbles answered with authority, "that she is screaming her head off."

Milo Perrier pulled his hands free and marched across to the still open-mouthed figure of the cook.

"What is it?" he asked her. "What has happened?"

The deaf-and-dumb girl managed at last to close her silently screaming mouth. She turned and pointed energetically in the direction of the kitchens.

"Is something wrong in kitchen?" asked Sidney Wang, who had come over to join Milo Perrier.

A quick dart of fear crossed Perrier's face.

"Something wrong?" he asked urgently. "With our dinner?"

Sam Diamond joined his fellow sleuths.

"Is someone in there, in the kitchen?" he asked.

Dick Charleston came across, too.

"Someone's in the kitchen with dinner?" he tried.

Sidney Wang stepped back a pace.

"Cook cannot hear or speak," he told them.

They looked at each other in dismay.

But all was not lost. The deaf-and-dumb girl was rummaging in her pocket. At last she pulled out a note typed on a small card. She handed it to Wang.

Wang read it aloud.

"It says this: 'I think the butler is dead. My name is Yetta. I don't work Thursdays. Signed: Acme Letter Writing Service.' "

"We must investigate this, Wang," Milo Perrier said. "Someone has to leave the room and go and see what has happened."

"Not someone," the Chinese sleuth answered. "Sometwo. Or maybe somethree."

The others took his point. This was not a night for anybody to be let out of sight on his own.

"Mr. Diamond, Mr. Charleston," Wang said, "you stay here with the others. Miss Marbles, Monsieur Perrier, and I will investigate."

But suddenly, as if in answer to his announcement, there came from behind the now shuttered tall windows a tremendous boom of thunder.

"Mr. Diamond," Milo Perrier said solemnly. "You have a gun. If necessary, use it."

"That'll be another ten bucks an hour, Frenchie," Sam said.

The three investigators gave him a combined glare of disapproval and turned to the open doorway.

Out in the hall the intrepid band made its way toward the kitchens and whatever was waiting there that had caused all that silent bawling.

Jessie Marbles, striding large-hipped down the length of the great hall with its silently watching suits of armor and terribly handy clusters of assorted weaponry, rubbed her hands briskly.

"At last," she said, her voice ringing cheerfully from the rafters high overhead. "At last a body. Something we can get our teeth into."

Wang and Perrier did not seem to feel that this was a remark in the best of taste, but duty called, and together all three continued their advance toward the baize-covered door leading down to the kitchen quarters. In silence they passed through it. A long bare corridor loomed in front of them. Casting occasional apprehensive glances from side to side, the two male sleuths followed the resoundingly heavy footsteps of their female colleague.

They came at last to the door of the kitchen. Wang stepped forward to push it politely open for Miss Marbles. He found it closed and reached for the doorknob.

"Stop," snapped Perrier.

115

Wang's hands froze above the knob.

"Fingerprints," Milo Perrier explained.

"Yours," said Perrier. "Here, take my—'ow you say?—handkerchief."

"*Mouchoir,*" muttered Wang, taking the carefully folded object the Belgian had proffered him.

He used it to turn the doorknob. Slowly the door creaked open. The three detectives crowded forward and peered in.

An astonishing sight met their eyes (was anything else to be expected?).

In a chair at the big table in the center of the big, old-fashioned kitchen sat Benson, the butler, but his head was slumped forward at an odd angle and at his side his arms dangled lifelessly.

The three sleuths cautiously crept toward him.

"Is he . . .?" asked Miss Marbles.

"He looks . . ." said Sidney Wang.

"Seems like . . ." Milo Perrier added.

Their joint perspicuity was marvelous. Very . . . indeed, Benson the butler appeared.

Sidney Wang stepped forward to pick up the slumped form.

"Stop," Milo Perrier said sharply.

Wang stopped.

"Touch nothing," Pierre commanded. "Fingerprints."

Wang assumed a wise expression.

"Quite so," he said. "Pencil!"

"Pencil!" Perrier said in his turn.

As one the two sleuths reached in their inner pockets. As one their hands emerged each holding a pencil with a neat india-rubber eraser top. As one, each reversed his pencil so that the eraser was to the fore. As one, they dipped toward the recumbent butler's head.

And as one each inserted the rubber tip of his pencil into an ear.

"One. Two. Three."

As one, they lifted. The head rose and then slumped backwards over the chair. The mouth was wide open. No one could have looked deader.

116

Sidney Wang took the limp wrist.

"No pulse," he announced. "No heartbeat. If condition does not change, this man is dead."

He let the limp wrist fall.

"Always was a bit limp-wristed, *ce* Benson," Perrier said in farewell.

He stooped and examined the body with care.

"No signs of foul play," he pronounced eventually.

"Hold on," said Miss Marbles. "What's this?"

She bent from her elephantine hips and sniffed carefully at a mug of brownish liquid on the kitchen table directly in front of the place where the butler was seated.

"What do you make of it, Perrier?" she asked.

The Belgian detective stooped and sniffed.

"Poison, *n'est-ce pas*?"

"No," said Jessie Marbles. "Not *n'est-ce pas*. Cocoa."

"So," Perrier said thoughtfully. "At last we have our murder."

But the Chinese sleuth shook his Oriental head in disagreement.

"Not quite," he said. "Mr. Twain say murder victim sitting at our table. Butler not at our table. Butler only killed to divert us from real murder still to come."

And, as if in instant confirmation of his words, Jessie Marbles, straightened from her inspection of the mysterious cocoa mug, saw something on the wall in front of her.

"Look!" she said.

On the wall where she was pointing there was a long rack of knives. It started with an itsy-bitsy little knife for paring very small oranges and ran all the way along to a great big knife for paring oranges about the size of hot-air balloons. The middle slot was empty.

"Twelve times with a butcher's knife," Jessie Marbles quoted softly.

"Eleven times with a butcher's knife," Milo Perrier quoted softly.

"Eleven, twelve, what difference?" Sidney Wang

misquoted softly. "What difference so long as is murder?"

Milo Perrier glanced quickly from side to side.

"That means the others are still in danger," he said. "Grave danger."

"What exact time, please?" Sidney Wang asked.

Perrier pulled out his watch and consulted it gravely. "Eleven thirty-one and fifty-six seconds."

"Twenty-eight minutes and no more till murder," Wang said.

"How time flies," Miss Marbles added, "when you're enjoying yourself."

But Wang was made of sterner stuff.

"Quickly," he said, his voice ringing with decision. "Everyone back into the dining room. Must all be together at midnight."

Jessie Marbles hastened to obey, but she was halted by Milo Perrier.

"One moment," he said in a voice ringing with yet more decision (no idiot of a Chinese was going to hog all the ringing voices).

He crossed quickly to the floggy form of Benson, the ex-butler. From a tightly clenched fist he extracted a small scrap of paper. With extreme care he unrolled it and smoothed it out.

"What is it?" Jessie Marbles asked, scarcely able to conceal her intense excitement.

"It is a bill," Perrier said, peering at the scrap. "Yes, everything here has been hired—'ow you say— rented for the night. The butler, the cook, the food, the extra dining room chairs . . . Everything."

"You mean . . .?" asked Miss Marbles, generously feeding him the punchline.

"Yes," he answered, accepting what was his due. "Yes, the entire murder has been catered."

13

If Lionel Twain was put out by his opponents' discovering how much of what lay in store for them was the result of artful arrangement, he was made fairly happy again when he heard through one of his multitude of microphones the words exchanged as the three sleuths paused in the lofty hall before reporting to their fellow guests inside the dining room the grim discovery that they had made.

"If you're right, Wang, about the main murder being still to come," Jessie Marbles pronounced, "there's still one thing to be said about the dead butler."

"And that is?" Milo Perrier asked.

"That Twain undoubtedly killed him," said Miss Marbles. "The man's mad."

A shiver disturbed the thick layer of tweed on her broad back.

"Mad, yes," agreed Milo Perrier. "But no fool. I only hope we are in time."

They all three hurried toward the dining room. Wang, the first to arrive, seized the handles of the heavy double doors and pulled. They resisted. He tugged harder. Still the doors remained obstinately closed.

Wang turned to the others with a puzzled frown.

"Locked," he said.

"Sam Diamond probably turned the key in the lock from the inside," Jessie Marbles answered. "He'd do that as a precaution."

Milo Perrier stepped up to the doors and knocked loudly.

"It's all right, Diamond," he called. "It is I, Milo Perrier. Open, please."

From the other side of the doors, utter silence.

Milo Perrier knocked again, yet more loudly.

"Diamond?" he called. "Charleston? Are you in there?"

From the far side of the doors, not a sound.

The detective trio looked at each other, not without nervousness. Milo Perrier raised his knuckles to the doors for a third time and knocked even more noisily.

Yet more profound silence.

"Diamond?" he called, almost frantic now. "Charleston? Diamond? Charleston?"

"Try Charleston Diamond," suggested Wang.

"Charleston? Diamond?"

He thundered on the doors.

And still there was not the least whisper of an answer.

"Quickly," Sidney Wang suggested, "go back to kitchen. Get dining room key from pocket of dead butler."

Perrier's egg-shaped face turned a pretty shade of green, somewhere between eau-de-Nil and olive with maybe a touch of emerald.

"You don't have to say 'dead butler,'" he expostulated. "It's bad enough I have to put my hand in his pocket."

But, brave little man, nevertheless he turned and set off again in the direction of the kitchens. Careless now of fingerprints and with the words "pocket," "dead," and "butler" thrusting themselves into his mind however often he thrust them out again, he seized the knob of the kitchen door and thrust it wide open.

A look of sheer horror spread itself across his egg-shaped face.

And, on the whole, it was justified.

Because there on the chair where hardly two minutes earlier the three of them had left the lifeless form of Benson the butler, now there were only his clothes. The correct black jacket, a spotless white shirt, the

120

correct striped trousers. The complete butler suit. There were two shoes on the floor just by the chair legs, correct black shoes. In them lay two socks, elegant black socks, one of which seemed to have been put on that morning the wrong way round (which, as everybody knows, is a fearfully unlucky thing to do).

Milo Perrier stared and stared at the bodiless garments. Slowly his lips formed some syllables.

"Holy *merde*!"

Meanwhile, back at the dining room doors Miss Marbles had taken over. Her decidedly formidable blood-red fist banged and thumped on the old mahogany.

"Miss Withers?" she called in stentorian tones. "Miss Skeffington?"

Bang, bang. Thump, thump.

The doors shook under the onslaught. Jessie Marbles had a fist that had tamed many a wild hen back in her quiet Sussex village.

Bang. Thump.

"Miss Skeffington? Miss Withers?"

Miss Marbles had a voice which often in an emergency had been borrowed by the Sussex coast guard on some particularly foggy night and had conveyed its warning to ships damn nearly into France.

But from behind these doors she got no answer at all.

Behind her Milo Perrier suddenly appeared. His egg-shaped face had gone from green to red, vermilion with touches of crimson, and here and there a trace of ruby.

Miss Marbles turned to him for the key to the doors. But all he could do was utter two words.

"He's gone!"

"Who's gone?" Jessie asked.

"The butler. His body is missing."

He unclenched his tightly clenched hand and produced the dining room doors key which he had found in the pocket of the butler's striped trousers, draped over the lower part of the chair on which his seemingly dead body had then been lying. He handed it to Sidney Wang.

121

Wang looked at the key and frowned, as much as any decently inscrutable Oriental could allow himself to.

"If butler gone," he asked, "where did you find key?"

"In his pocket," Perrier replied tersely.

"What pocket?" Jessie Marbles asked in mystification.

"The butler's pocket," Perrier answered, reluctant to come out with the full details of such an apparently ridiculous event.

"Butler gone, but pocket still there?" Wang asked, getting moment by moment more bewildered.

"Exactly," said Perrier, nerving himself up to the revelation at last. "Somebody has stolen his body but left his—'ow you say—clothes."

"Left his—'ow you say—clothes?" Jessie Marbles asked. "Positively weird. Who would want a naked dead body?"

Sidney Wang and Milo Perrier gave each other long cautious looks.

"Are you," Perrier said slowly, "thinking what . . ."

"*Oooh la la!*" Perrier answered. "Crazy, but *ooh la la!*"

"Yes," said Wang.

A look of sharp determination came over Jessie Marbles' battle-ax features.

"Quickly," she said to Wang, as he stood there thinking hard and holding the key Perrier had handed over to him. "Quickly, open these doors. Something's very wrong here!"

Hastily Wang pushed the key into the keyhole. With sweat-slippery fingers he wrenched it around. He yanked at the doorknob. His sweaty palms failed to turn it. He wiped his hand angrily on his magnificent Chinese evening robe. He tried the doorknob again. And this time he succeeded in getting it to turn. He flung wide both the double doors in a single movement.

The three detectives stood aghast.

Their worst forebodings about their unanswered knocking and shouting were realized. But not in a way that any of them, had they thought about it for the rest of the night, could possibly have imagined.

The dining room had not been turned into a slaughterhouse of dead bodies. The guests of Lionel Twain were not lying gagged and bound where they had last seen them.

They were simply not there at all.

Everything in the big dining room was exactly as it had been when the three of them had set out on their expedition to the kitchens to see what it was that had so alarmed the deaf-and-dumb Yetta. But there was not the least trace of any human being there.

The old oak-paneled walls looked down on the long, long dining table with its fine white cloth just as they had been doing not fifteen minutes earlier. The clock on the wall still ticked and tocked inexorably the minutes remaining before the hour of midnight. The moose head above the mantelpiece still regarded the scene below with moth-eaten mooseness. The soup plates in front of each place were still as empty as when Benson, who should perhaps be called the late Benson, had attempted with singular lack of success to pour into them the first course of the promised dinner (which certainly should be called the late dinner). Even the hole in the cloth in front of Wang's seat was still there.

But of Dick Charleston and of Dora Charleston; of Sam Diamond, the tough; and of Tess, the been-around; of faithful *secrétaire*-cum-chauffeur Marcel; of gently slumbering Miss Withers; of wide-awake Number Three adopted Son, Willie, there was neither hide nor hair. Nor was there of Yetta, the cook, deaf, dumb and now quite gone.

Slowly the three sleuths advanced into the empty room.

"Hello?" Jessie Marbles called in the voice the Sussex coast guard so liked to employ. "Hello? Where is everyone?"

But she knew that it was useless.

"Room is filled with empty people," remarked Wang with all the wisdom of the East.

But not all the wisdom of the East could alter the plain fact staring them in the face.

"I'll try the other door," Milo Perrier said.

He set off toward it, but something in the slump of his shoulders indicated that when he opened the door he did not really expect to find the seven missing guests lined up outside waiting to come back in.

When he tried the door, he found that it was locked. His eyes flew down to the keyhole. And there in it was the key.

"Locked," he told the others. "Locked and from the inside."

Sidney Wang put on an expression of deep thoughtfulness. There was little else he could do, but there were times when he got tired of Oriental inscrutability.

"Both doors locked from inside," he said, "yet no way out."

Milo Perrier turned from his inspection of the door. "I don't like it," he said. "I don't like it one bit."

Well, someone had to say that before the case was over, and Milo Perrier was determined to get all the best lines for himself.

"I like it," Sidney Wang retorted, "but don't understand it."

Point to me, he thought.

"In all my years," Jessie Marbles pronounced, "this is the second strangest thing I've ever seen."

"What was the first?" Perrier asked helpfully.

"Somebody making off with a dead blind naked butler."

The three of them looked around the big empty room again in sheer dismay. But Sidney Wang was not beaten yet. A look of cunning came into his eyes. Rapidly he crossed to the nearest section of the oak paneling and with expert fingers he began to examine every inch of it.

"Maybe another way out of room," he said. "Secret passageway, perhaps."

A glint of hope lit up the eyes of Miss Marbles and Milo Perrier. Of course, a secret passage. Hadn't they had scores of them in earlier cases? Perhaps in the less memorable days of their first adventures when the art was still a bit primitive, but they had them all right. And, by golly, if they've got them again now, they know how to deal with them. (You feel with expert fingers till you encounter a slight projection in a part of the paneling; you press on it; the seemingly solid panel yields; a small cavity is revealed; without a second thought—and certainly not leaving a note to your official police colleague—you plunge down the narrow passage; you are caught by the villains at the far end; your life is in imminent danger; with one bound you are free. Easy.)

But in an instant hope was shattered.

From somewhere up above them a voice boomed out. It was recognizable instantly. The voice of their friendly host, Lionel Twain.

"Wrong," it said flatly. "No secret passageways, Mr. Wang."

Sidney Wang wheeled round.

"There," he said. "Voice come from cow on wall."

"Moose!" screamed the voice from the moth-eaten head. "Moose! Moose! Moose! You imbecile!"

But if Lionel Twain (or the moose) could shout in anger, so could somebody else.

Milo Perrier planted himself in front of the head and delivered his broadside. (His broad side was his front side. He was a tubby little gourmand.)

"Where are they?" he demanded. "What have you done with the others, you minuscule madman?"

"Aha," said the moose gleefully. "Stumped already? Need some *clues, Monsieur* Perrier?"

"Clues?" he yelled. "I find my own clues. I need no clues from you, you deranged lollipop."

Sidney Wang laid a restraining hand on his colleague's chubby shoulder.

"Calm yourself," he advised. "Man who argues with moose head is like train without wheels. Very soon get nowhere."

Perrier wheeled round, his face still boiling and bubbling with passion.

"Oh, be quiet," he snapped. "I am sick of your— 'ow you say—fortune cookies."

"Man who is sick of—'ow you say—fortune cookies

—" Wang began. But Perrier interrupted him savagely.

"What?" he screamed. "Another one?"

"Sssh, gentlemen, please," coaxed Jessie Marbles.

But, well launched into a fortune cookie motto, Sidney Wang was a hard man to stop. And the thought of one missed opportunity already this evening, the matter of treacherous roads and fresh mushrooms, still rankled.

He took a deep breath.

"Man who is sick of fortune cookies," he repeated with tremendous emphasis.

"Man who is sick in head goes on and on about fortune cookies," Milo Perrier jumped in.

"Man who has egg-shaped head," Wang retorted, "like lady with bell-bottom trousers he—"

"Lady with—'ow you say—bell-bottom trousers is neither here nor there," Perrier countered. "Never, I tell you, in all my cases—"

"Man with many cases like engineer with four thumbs. He—"

"And I have never encountered anywhere an engineer with four—'ow you say—thumbs. And If I did—"

"Ah ha, ha," said a moose-like voice from above.

They ceased in an instant and turned to glower at the moth-eaten headpiece.

"Aha," it said, "dissension in the ranks."

It paused and cleared its moose-like throat as if about to recite a poem.

And the reason for that immediately became obvious.

"(Cough, cough)" it said.

> "One more murder still to come.
> Don't know when I've had such fun."

Jessie Marbles looked up at the moose with a severe schoolmistress glare.

"And we can do without any inane couplets," she said. "Now then, 'fess up (as they say in these parts). What have you done with the others?"

"In need of a hint, Miss Marbles?" came the irritating voice of the moose. "Tch, tch, how surprising. But if you insist . . ."

Again the moth-eaten head cleared its moth-eaten

throat as if about to recite a poem. And again it was.

"Cough, cough)

"You all mistake what you assume;
They never left the dining room,
Count the numbers one to ten;
Turn the knob and try again."

Highly delighted with its poetic effort, the moose indulged in a prolonged fit of high-pitched giggles.

But at last even he had had enough self-congratulation. Abruptly the all-too-human eyes in the moth-eaten head disappeared instantly to be replaced with all-too-moose-like ones.

"What the devil does that mean?" Jessie Marbles asked. "The fellow can't even rhyme. 'They never left the dining rhume indeed. Well, they *did* for one thing."

"Do not mistake what you *assoom,* Miss Marbles," Sidney Wang said. "Quick, back out in hall."

"What for?" Perrier asked, a little cross at not having issued the command himself.

"We may assume others not here," Wang replied, "but moose say they *are* in dining room. Let us look once more."

Milo Perrier shrugged. Well, you have to go out of your way to humor these crazy foreigners.

Miss Marbles shrugged. Not a very English way of tacklin' a case, but . . .

They went back out into the hall.

"Please close doors, *Monsieur* Perrier," Wang said.

Carefully Milo Perrier reclosed the doors that he had flung open to reveal that disconcertingly empty room. He gave another shrug, a real old Gallic one starting from the soles of his feet.

"I cannot see what possible good . . ." he said.

"Quiet, please," said Wang.

He had been counting under his breath. But now he allowed them to listen in, generous fellow.

". . . six, seven, eight, nine, ten."

He let out a long breath.

"Miss Marbles," he said, "you be so kind to open doors, please."

Jessie Marbles looked at him the way an English lady of class looks at a foreigner (down her nose). But she could think of nothing else to do, so she turned and flung the door wide again. Her mouth dropped wide, wide open in amazement.

Around the long table in the old dining room were seated Sam Diamond, San Francisco investigator, and Tess Skeffington, his secretary and—well, you know what. With them are Dick Charleston, of New York, Palm Springs, and Beverly Hills, with Dora, his delightful (and rich, thank goodness) wife, and Willie Wang, Number Three Son, adopted, of ace investigator Sidney Wang, and Nurse Withers (still asleep) and Marcel Cassette, *secrétaire*-cum-chauffeur. And seated nearby was Yetta, deaf-and-dumb maid with a pocketful of cards for all occasions from the Acme Letter Writing Service.

Just exactly as they had been when the trio outside had left them.

14

As the three sleuths came dazedly into the so suddenly repeopled dining room, Sam Diamond looked up from his place at the table.

"Where were you, Wang? he asked, in a slightly anxious tone. "We was worried."

"What do you mean, where were we?" Jessie Marbles instantly retorted. "Where were *you*?"

Dick Charleston looked at her in some surprise.

"We were here," he answered mildly. "Didn't you say not to leave the dining room?"

Milo Perrier stepped forward, intelligence glowing on every inch of his egg-shaped face. This is the man who solved the mystery of the two-headed capitalist, the strange affair of the South Mersea Dinosaur, the matter of the Crown Prince of Lower Bosno-Silesia's cufflinks and the Adventure of the Duchess's Upper Teeth.

"And you have not been out of this room since we were gone?" he asked with incisive sharpness.

"Certainly not," Dick Charleston replied, still mildly puzzled at the unexpected attitude of his returned colleagues.

"Very easy answer," commented Sidney Wang. "But question very hard."

Sam Diamond remembered the original reason for the sortie the three had made.

"Where's the butler?" he inquired.

"The butler?" Milo Perrier answered in a tone of the utmost solemnity. "*Il est mort.*"

"Mort?" Sam asked, bewildered. "Who the heck's Mort?"

But to Dora Charleston, a woman of the world, the subtleties of the French language presented little or no obstacle.

"The butler's dead?" she asked.

"Butler completely murdered," Sidney Wang confirmed.

"Poisoned," added Milo Perrier. "Yet a butcher's knife was missing there."

"We came back here to inform you," Jessie Marbles explained. "But the doors were locked."

"I went back to get the key out of the butler's pocket," Milo Perrier went on, deciding that he might as well produce all the unlikely details in one batch. "But when I got there, I found that the butler's body was missing. He had been stripped naked and his clothes had been left behind in his place."

Dora Charleston shook her pretty head dazedly.

"I don't understand," he said. "Why would anyone steal a dead naked body?"

Dick Charleston leaned toward her.

"Well, sometimes, dear," he began, "people . . ."

The rest of his words were lost in a whisper. It was a fairly long whisper. As he proceeded, Dora's eyes grew wider. And wider. And wider and wider and wider.

"Oh, that's *tacky*!" she exclaimed at last. "That's *really* tacky!"

But Jessie Marbles was not one to be put off by incidental details, however tacky. Sternly she returned to the subject at hand.

"Then when *Monsieur* Perrier had found the clothes without the body," she said, "and had come back with the key to the locked doors, we opened them. But the room was completely empty. You had all gone, every man jack of you!"

Every man jack of them looked at every other man jack of them. They seemed to be all present and correct.

130

"The moose head there," Jessie Marbles went on, daring them to disbelieve, "told us not to *assoom* you *had* left the *rhume*. So we counted to ten and tried again. And here you all were."

She looked around at them, searchingly.

"I'm not one to use hyperbole, ladies and gentlemen," she added, even pronouncing the word right. "But I'll tell you this. For the first time in my life I've had the ka-ka scared out of me."

"I like her," Dora said confidently to Tess Skeffington. "I really like her."

But . . .

Suddenly two gunshots rang out. They seemed to come from the direction of the kitchen.

"Gunshots, Pop," Willie Wang instantly informed his respected father.

"Gunshots, *monsieur*," Marcel simultaneously informed his respected employer.

"Gunshots, Sam," Tess no less quickly informed her respected—well, you know what.

"Gunshots, Dickie," Dora informed her respectable husband. (Well, marry enough money and you get to be respectable.)

"Gzzz shzzz," Nurse Withers instantly (or not absolutely instantly) snored to her respected employer.

The sleuths accepted and digested the information, Milo Perrier reflecting that this was the only thing he had gotten to digest so far on this accursed evening.

Sam Diamond was the first to translate reflection into action. Perhaps this was because he was translating from American into American, possessing the inestimable advantage of speaking only those two lanuages.

"This time," he said, "Charleston and I will go investigate. Everyone else wait in this room."

Dick Charleston moved to join Sam at the door. Sidney Wang took a quick look at the ticktocking clock.

"Be careful, Diamond," he warned. "Only ten more minutes before next murder."

"I know the schedule," Sam answered, petulantly rounding on him.

He gave him a reassuring slap on the shoulder. "C'mon, buddy," he said. "Let's go."

The two of them left at a run, banging the double doors closed behind them.

The others looked at each other.

"What do you make of all this, Wang?" Milo Perrier asked confidentially.

Sidney Wang devoted himself to thought. After a very short while, however, he came up with an answer.

"Is confusing."

"IT. IT. IT IT IT."

The voice of the moose head was heard in the land. And it was a pretty irritating voice, too.

"IT is confusing," it went on. "It. It. It. Say your goddam pronouns, can't you!"

Meanwhile, out in the long, long corridor approaching the kitchen of the old house Sam Diamond and Dick Charleston were quickly but cautiously making their way toward the shut door of the kitchen. As they got near it, Sam pulled out his gun.

They crept the last few yards. Dick reached forward and grasped the doorknob. He looked at Sam. Sam looked at the door. He took a new grip of the gun in his hand. He gave Dick a nod.

Dick jerked the knob around and hurled the door open. Sam leaped forward in a gunfighter's crouch.

"Good God!" said Dick.

"What is it?" Sam asked, too busy with his gunfighter's crouch, which he thought he did pretty well, to have bothered much with anything inside the kitchen.

"He's back!" Dick said in answer.

And, true enough, once more the butler was lying in just the position in which Miss Marbles, Sidney Wang, and Milo Perrier had first discovered him. He was slumped in the chair drawn up to the big table, lying with his head on the side on the table with his arms dangling.

But there was one difference from his previous appearance.

A pretty startling difference.

He was stark, staring naked. He was as nude as a

132

stripper at the end of her act. He was wearing, to put it another way, nothing but his birthday suit. He was starkers. He was bare, stripped to the buff, in a state of nature, in—to make things crystal clear—*puris naturalibus*. Unclad.

Sam Diamond strode over.

"I don't get it," he said. "I just don't get it. First they steal the body and leave the clothes . . . Then they steal the clothes and leave the body. Who would do a thing like that?"

"Possibly," suggested Dick, racking his detective brains, "some deranged dry-cleaner?"

"And what about the gunshots?" Sam asked. "Why shoot some poor slob who's already been poisoned?"

"True," Dick replied. "We heard gunshots, all right, but I see no bullet holes."

He peered at the naked butler from all angles, craning over him, crouching to see as far under him as he could, twisting and turning.

"Not on his head or neck or back or chest," he concluded.

"Look all over him," Sam said tersely, and through tight lips.

"All over his body?" Dick asked, giving Sam a highly suspicious look.

"Somebody has to do it," Sam replied. "I'm busy."

"Busy?" Dick raised his eyebrows.

Sam flourished the forty-five.

"Somebody has to stand guard, don't they?" he said.

Dick frowned.

"But why don't I stand guard and you look all over?" he suggested at last.

Sam pondered, through tight lips.

"All right," he said eventually. "We'll take turns. You look all over the first dead naked body we find, and I'll take the second one. But hurry up. We only got eight minutes left."

Dick glared at him. Fair play was all very well, but not when it meant . . .

Sam looked at him grimly. Fair play was fair play. And somebody's gotta keep guard.

Such thoughts ran through his mind, as he stood

tensely on the watch. Let anyone try coming in and disturbing things and, boy, just watch out. Let 'em come, that's all. Let 'em . . .

"Finished?" he asked. "See anything?"

"There's not a single bullet hole on this ma—"

Dick stopped abruptly.

"I see something," Dick's voice came, muffledly.

Sam's ears pricked up.

"What is it?"

Silence.

Muffled silence.

"Forget it," Dick said at last.

He straightened up.

"My mistake," he apologized. "It—it wasn't a bullet hole."

Sam's face took on a puzzled frown.

"If he wasn't slugged," he asked loudly, "why the shots?"

"Divide and conquer," answered Dick.

Sam's face took on a doubly puzzled frown.

"Whazzat?"

"Another diversion," Dick explained patiently as he could. "To separate us. Twain can't possibly take on the five of us all at once, so his plan is to separate us as much as possible."

Understanding began to dawn on Sam's face. Dick continued.

"He gives us meaningless clues to confuse us, dangles red herrings before our eyes, bedazzles us with bizarre banalities while all the precious seconds tick away toward the truly terrible murder still to come."

Sam's eyes were open wide in admiration now.

"You're good, Charleston," he said. "You're not my kinda cop but you're smart."

He paused.

"And you smell good," he added. "You're not a pansy, I know that, but what the hell are you?"

Dick shrugged modestly.

"Classy, I suppose," he suggested.

"Dames always go for a guy like you, don't they?" Sam asked with wistfulness.

"I can't see what possible interest . . ." Dick replied, stiffening.

"Ever make it with a waitress?" Sam asked.

"I beg your pardon."

"A waitress? A big, fat waitress. I don't know what them society ladies are like in the kip, but you ain't never had it till you made it with a big, fat waitress. If you're ever interested, give me a call."

He swung away, ashamed of the intimate secrets he had been letting fall to this newfound friend, and started back toward the dining room, gun at the ready.

"Bizarre little twit," Dick Charleston murmured to himself as he prepared to follow.

"I'm still not sure about that guy," Sam murmured to himself as he led the way.

They reached the immense hallway again. Suddenly Dick Charleston, who had taken the lead, came to a halt. Slowly his hand reached out to the knob of a small door just beside him.

"What . . . what are you doing?" Sam Diamond whispered, taking a firmer grip of his gun.

Dick gave him a pallid smile.

"I'm going in here to wash my hands," he said. "You know, after . . ."

Sam nodded in understanding.

"I'll go ahead and tell the others just what's happened in there."

Dick entered the bathroom.

Sam Diamond made his way back to the dining room, looking cautiously around at every inch of the way. But nothing seemed to disturb the calm of the big old house.

He reached the dining room and strode rapidly in.

"Well," he said, "you're never gonna believe this, but—"

He stopped short and looked all around about him in sheer thunderstruck amazement.

15

The dining-room, which Sam Diamond had entered confident that he was about to do no more than give his fellow guests the bizarre news of the latest developments in the case of the disappearing butler, his disappearing body, his disappearing clothes, and his reappearing body, was totally and utterly empty. The table was there as before, the chairs around it were in just the positions they would have been in if Lionel Twain's guests had been sitting awaiting the long, long delayed arrival of something to eat. But there was no more trace of a person than there had been when Miss Marbles, Sidney Wang, and Monsieur Perrier had returned some twenty minutes earlier.

Sam walked cautiously farther into the empty, hollowly echoing room.

"Awright," he said through tight lips, "where are you?"

He ducked down and glared suspiciously under the long table with its heavy white damask cloth. Nothing there.

"What the hell's going on here?" he asked himself, straightening up.

He marched back toward the far door and called out, his voice ringing mysteriously in the high-raftered room.

"Hey, Charleston! Wash up later. We got problems."

But no answer came from the hall where moments

137

earlier he had left Dick Charleston to wash his hands after—after what he had had to do investigating the naked body of the butler for possible bullet holes.

Sam crossed the big room in a few strides and seized the knob of the far door. It was locked.

"Locked from the inside," he said to himself through tight lips. "That can mean only one thing—and I don't know what that is."

He yelled out once more.

"Charleston!"

But still Dick Charleston did not come to his aid. He wheeled on his heel and went back down the length of the dining room and out into the hall. He crossed to the bathroom door, almost at a run.

He jerked it open.

"You're never gonna believe what I—"

His voice came to a flat stop.

The bathroom in front of him was as completely and totally empty as the dining room behind him.

He gave it a long, hard, penetrating survey. And at once it was evident that the little room had no other way out. There was a window, but thick and rust-coated iron bars prevented anyone from getting out that way. Otherwise the room contained only a toilet and a washbasin. And there was not even any water in the basin.

Thoughtfully Sam Diamond closed the door. But he was unable immediately to fix on any course of action. Thoughtfully he opened the door again, unable to believe what his eyes told him.

And he found himself looking into the Charlestons' bedroom, a room that ought to have been somewhere up on the floor above. On a chair from which a thick layer of dust, or baking flour, had been removed lay Dick Charleston's coat. Scattered here and there in high profusion were Dora Charleston's knickknacks and fal-lals, a knickknack there, a fal-lal here. On the bed was Myron, licking a sugar cobweb.

At the sight of the intruder Myron raised himself up and uttered a low deep menacing growl. Sam hastily closed the door.

"Interesting case," he said, through tight lips.

138

He turned, thinking deeply, and made his way back to the door of the dining room. It was closed.

"Funny," he muttered. "I don't remember closing this door . . ."

From the holster under his armpit he took his trusty forty-five. Very cautiously he put out his left hand to the knob of the door. Very, very cautiously he twisted it. No watcher on the far side unless he was crouching over the knob keeping the closest guard, could possibly have told that it was being turned. At last it was fully around. Sam paused and took a deep breath. He glanced down at the snub-nosed forty-five in his right hand. All ready.

He braced himself and flung the door wide.

Around the long table in the dining room all Lionel Twain's guests, with the exception of Dick Charleston, were peacefully sitting.

Sam, gun in hand, stood at the flung-open door and blinked.

"What happened?" Milo Perrier asked him.

"Yes," said Miss Marbles, "what were the gunshots?"

"I'm hungry, Sam," Tess Skeffington complained. "Can't we get a hamburger some place?"

Sam just stood there and blinked.

Sidney Wang smiled a grave Oriental smile.

"So it happened to you?" he said to Sam, mindful of his own Oriental bewilderment when he had found the dining room empty and then after a count of ten full again.

But Dora Charleston had a more urgent question.

"Where's my Dickie?"

Every face at once turned to her. A deep blush swept over her pretty face.

"Sorry," she gulped. "I mean, where's my husband?"

Sam slowly shook his head from side to side.

"Wait a minute," he said. "Wait a minute, something isn't kosher here. I'm gonna try this again, and nobody move."

He stepped back outside and carefully closed the door. In the hallway, watched with sardonic amusement by a dozen or more suits of armor in most of which were concealed TV cameras, he began solemnly counting.

"One—two—three—I feel like a freakin' fruitcake —five—six—seven—countin' like this, and through tight lips, too—eight—nine—*ten!*"

He seized the doorknob, yanked it around and hurled the door wide open.

He found himself looking into the bathroom where Dick Charleston had gone to wash his hands after that unfortunate episode. Dick, at the basin busy with the soap, turned his head and glanced at him more than a little sourly.

"I said I'll be out in a minute," he barked.

Sam looked at him wonderingly. Through tight lips, he heaved a great sigh of mystification. Then he slammed the door in a sudden burst of frustrated rage, took a heavy hip flask out of his pocket, put it to his lips, and threw back his head. The prolonged gurgling sound that followed had scarcely finished when the door behind him cautiously opened. Milo Perrier was standing there, with—at his back and looking distinctly curious—all the rest of Lionel Twain's guests except the one person Sam believed to be in that room —only he believed it was a washroom—Dick Charleston.

"Well?" Milo Perrier asked. "Are you going to come back in or are you not?"

Dazedly Sam walked back into the dining room. He looked around at the long table, the chairs, the moose head over the mantelpiece, the big old clock ticktocking away, the seated figure of deaf-and-dumb Yetta, as if he was totally unable to credit what his eyes were telling him.

"It happened again," he said after a long, long while.

"What happened, Sam?" Tess asked dutifully.

"Ten seconds ago," Sam replied, hammering the words out through tight lips, "I walked in and this room was a toilet."

"Who you see in the toilet?" Sidney Wang asked.

"Dick Charleston," Sam replied.

"You could at least have knocked," Dora rebuked him.

But there was one of the circle who was ready with a rebuke of another sort. Jessie Marbles coughed sharply.

"Two minutes to midnight," she said in a voice frost-edged as a winter lawn. "In case anyone is interested."

But Sam had had too much of a shock even to heed the voice of his buddy of old.

"It ain't possible, I'm telling you," he persisted. "Eight people in a dining room can't turn into a toilet unless ... ."

His voice trailed away.

"Unless what, Sam?" asked the well-trained Tess.

But it was not Sam who answered. It was Sidney Wang.

"Unless," he said, "it never happened."

Milo Perrier chipped in quickly. If astonishing revelations were being bandied out, he was not going to be left out.

"I see your point, Diamond," he said loudly. "When is a dining room filled with people not a dining room filled with people?"

"When," said Jessie Marbles triumphantly, "it is two dining rooms."

"Exactly," Sam confirmed.

"Two dining rooms?" Dora asked, still sweetly bewildered as ever.

"Two dining rooms," Wang explained. "Two toilets. Two of everything. Mr. Twain is an electronic genius."

"He has devised a way," Perrier added, "for this room to move swiftly and silently in the flash of an eye to be replaced by a exact duplicate of this very room."

Young Willie Wang grinned broadly.

"I knew it all the time," he claimed.

Milo Perrier ignored him. This was men's stuff, between detectives only.

"I shall demonstrate," he announced. "I shall go out of that—'ow you say?—door, close it, knock three times, and you shall all be gone. Observe!"

He marched across to the door, went through it and closed it with scrupulous care behind him.

Inside, they all listened.

In a moment three loud knocks came on the door. It opened, and in walked Dick Charleston.

"I've got it all figured out," he announced cheerfully. "There are two of everything."

"Oh, Dickie," Dora said in disappointment. "That's old news."

Dick looked hurt.

"Everyone here?" he asked, with some anxiety.

"All except Perrier," Jessie Marbles answered. "I'll wager he's in what you Americans will insist on calling the bathroom."

Sidney Wang sent a sharp glance over toward the big clock inexorably ticking out the seconds on the wall above them.

"One minute to midnight," he said warningly. "If Perrier not come back, he may be murder victim."

From her wheelchair the voice of the snoozing Nurse Withers raised itself momentarily.

"Murder-poo?"

Jessie Marbles went and patted her comfortingly.

"Any moment now, dear," she said.

Nurse Withers loosed off a fit of pleasurable giggles.

Sam Diamond strode to the center of the stage.

"All right, everybody take a seat," he commanded, through tight lips.

"I'm scared, Sam," Tess said. "Hold me."

"Hold yourself," he retorted with extraordinary speed.

He turned to the others again, fresh commands ready at the brim of his tight lips.

"The same seats you had before," he ordered.

His order was obeyed. Each of them went toward a chair. Jessie Marbles casting an extremely anxious glance up toward the big clock.

"Thirty seconds," she said with a little shiver. "I'm really very worried about *Monsieur* Perrier."

Nor was she the only one. The faithful Marcel might not have been very talkative in the company of his

142

betters, but he had been worrying away like a demented spaniel ever since his master had left them.

And now he broke down.

He swung around from the chair he had been heading toward.

"I'm going back to look for—'ow you say—*Monsieur* Perrier," he declared.

"Sit, please," shouted Sidney Wang, his voice cutting through the tense air. "No one to leave room!"

But, while Marcel was hovering indecisively, torn between his desire to see for himself his beloved master and his instinct to do what he had been told since he had been told it good and loudly, suddenly in the silence of the long room there sounded three loud knocks.

They did not, however, come from the door toward which Marcel was heading. They came from the door at the other end.

Everybody wheeled around and stared at that far door.

Marcel rushed—clump, clump, clump in his chauffeur's boots—down the length of the room and seized the knob of the door.

And all the while the big old clock was signaling that it was nearer and nearer the fatal moment. *Tick. Tick. Tick.*

Marcel tried to tear the door open. It resisted.

"It is locked," he called out. "I cannot open it."

"Hurry, man," Jessie Marbles boomed. "We have precisely twelve seconds."

Tick, tock. Tick, tock.

Marcel struggled and struggled with the locked door. His sweaty hands slipped and slid on the unyielding knob. Perspiration broke out on his forehead. His boots drummed on the floor.

Tick. Tock. Tick. Tock.

Suddenly a shadow loomed behind him.

"Here," said a voice, through tight lips, "let me."

Sam Diamond once again hauled the forty-five out of its shoulder holster. He stepped up and held the barrel close against the lock. His finger tightened. There was a heavy click. He swore and released the safety

catch. His finger tightened again. There was the re-
sounding noise of a shot. The lock flew away in
splinters.

Marcel tugged the door open like a man demented.

Milo Perrier was standing there.

He was wearing the butler's uniform.

It did not fit all that well. Milo Perrier was a good
deal stouter than Benson. Too many cups of hot chocolate and too many carefully thought-out dinners had
seen to that. But somehow or other the butler's suit,
correct black jacket, correct striped trousers, white
shirt, black socks, had got around the Perrier frame.
And somehow or other the butler's dark glasses had
got themselves across the pudgy Perrier nose. And
somehow or other the butler's white cane was dangling
by its strap from his wrist.

"Do not ask me," he begged simply.

"What are you doing in the butler's uniform?" Dick
Charleston asked at once.

"I said don't ask me."

But the rage left his egg-shaped face as quickly as it
had come. A sheerly woebegone expression replaced
it.

"I don't know how," he said. "It all happened too—
'ow you say—fast."

But this transformation of sleuth into butler was not
to be the only surprise of these few seconds. Sam
Diamond had been the first able to take his eyes off the
astonishing sight of Milo Perrier, and as he had done
so he had discovered that something else had happened.

His voice rose to a near-hysterical note as, through
tight lips, he spoke.

"The cook! Where's the cook?"

They all spun round to look at the chair where until
that instant Yetta had been sitting tranquilly deaf and
dumb.

She was no longer there.

"She's gone," said Tess, putting into words what they
all were feeling.

"Never said a thing," Dora added sadly.

144

But this was no time for sentiment or for recalling old friends.

"Five more seconds," Jessie Marbles announced in her friend of the Sussex coast guard voice. "Five more seconds! Quickly! Sit and join hands!"

There was a tremendous scramble for places around the table. Anyone might have thought that the grand old Christmas game of musical chairs was being played. But there were chairs and chairs enough for all who would sit at the table. If someone was going to be removed, it would not be because they were unable to find a place to plump down when the music stopped.

"Impossible for murder to happen now without witnesses," Sidney Wang triumphantly proclaimed as he took the last place.

All eyes fastened on the clock.

"Three," counted Jessie Marbles, just in case anyone was not too good at telling the time. "Two. One."

The clock slowly began to chime out the midnight hour.

One. Two. Three. Four.

Faces round the table looked terrified of what might happen on the final stroke.

Five. Six. Seven. Nine. (No, hold it, hold it.) Eight.

The tension grew. Sticky palm was clutched on sticky palm.

Eight. (No, get it right.) Nine. Ten. Eleven. Twelve.

The last chime died away into the still air.

"It's over," proclaimed Jessie Marbles, breathing out a sigh of relief so puffy that it blew up the white tablecloth in front of her.

"It's over. We're safe and sound."

But . . .

But suddenly . . .

But suddenly on the great double doors of the big high old room there came, one by one, hammering and reverberating, three loud knocks.

Dora smiled palely.

She gulped.

"It's probably the cook," she said.

She turned toward the doors and called out.

"Come in!"

"Darling," said Dick, "the poor woman is stone deaf."

"Sorry, I forgot," Dora said.

She took in a huge breath, filling her lungs to the last cubic inch.

"Come in," she screamed.

The doors remained shut. But the cook's deafness was not the only possible reason for that. Sidney Wang had thought of another.

"Do not believe it is cook," he said.

He rose from his chair.

"Excuse, please."

He went over to the doors. Every pair of eyes was on him. He reached the doors. He took hold of the knob of each in either hand. He tugged. The doors flew open.

Lionel Twain was standing there, pink tuxedo and all. His face was wearing a big, big smile.

"Ah, Mr. Twain," Wang said, with Oriental impassivity.

He stepped back half a pace.

"It seems," he said, still addressing his broadly smiling host, "that you were wrong about one of us around table being murdered. Won't you come in?"

He stepped back another half pace and ushered forward the diminutive pink-tuxedoed figure.

Still with that broad, broad smile on his face, Lionel Twain slowly pitched forward and flopped straight onto the floor.

A big butcher's knife was protruding from his back.

16

The lofty old dining room rang and rang with screams, women's screams.

Tess Skeffington was screaming. Dora Charleston was screaming. Nurse Withers was snoring in a scream-like way.

Lionel Twain was dead—stabbed in the back with a big, keen-bladed butcher's knife, and it was enough to cause any woman to scream after the slow ordeal of waiting for the promised midnight hour to strike and the way it had apparently struck without a murder having taken place.

So the women, except for Jessie Marbles, who had seen far too many corpses in a lifetime of investigation starting way back in the black-and-white days, if not even in the pretalkies era, had screamed.

But no one can keep screaming forever. So at last Dora Charleston stopped.

"Is . . . is he dead?" she asked as soon as she had breath enough.

"With a thing like that in his back," Sam Diamond answered, "in the long run he's better off."

But now, the screaming part done, the five detectives moved forward to kneel beside the body and examine it. In some cases "closely" and in others "with the eyes that missed nothing."

"Do not touch anything," Milo Perrier warned them sharply.

Jessie Marbles rounded on him. She had had difficulty getting down in any case, and it had done nothing for her temper.

"Will you stop saying 'Do not touch anything,'" she roared. "We're all experienced criminologists, aren't we? And personally, I find it insulting, debasing, and redundant for you to keep telling us not to touch anything."

"Be quiet, woman," Perrier replied.

Gone was the famed Continental courtesy. Not a hint of *"Je m'excuse, madame"* or "If you will forgive me, but . . ." It was the plain unvarnished jibe and nothing else.

Elderly lady criminologists are not the only ones who find it difficult to kneel down beside a corpse. Elderly gentlemen criminologists find it equally tough on their elderly joints. And, besides, hadn't he been saying "Do not touch anything" for scores of years as he had knelt beside a corpse? So why in the name of—'ow you say?—tarnation should he stop saying it now?

But he got more than he bargained for by way of reply.

"Up yours, fella," said Jessie Marbles of Sussex, England, spinster.

"Most amusing," growled Sidney Wang.

He too had not exactly found it easy to bend the Chinese knees to get down beside the corpse. And he too had knelt beside more corpses than you could count on the fingers of one computer since he had begun in the business and in consequence his temper, too, was more than a little frayed around its Oriental edges.

"Most amusing. Bickering detectives like making giant lamb stew. Everything going to pot."

And, as one, all four great sleuths rounded on him for that.

"Shut him up."

"Knock it off."

"We've had enough of you."

"'Ow you say—*taisez-vous.*"

"Can it, can't you?"

"Put a sock in it, you Chinese cracky-knees."

148

But the hubbub was suddenly silenced. By a gun-shot.

Sam Diamond had pulled the forty-five from his shoulder holster (again!) and fired a shot into the ceiling high above them. It was a good way of obtaining a hearing.

Into the sudden silence Sam spoke, through tight lips.

"Shut up, all of youse. Nobody move. Stay where you are, everyone."

The detectives froze. After all, a forty-five speaks loud and clear, and certainly Sam Diamond had a deadly determined look on his face.

"What is it?" Dick Charleston asked tensely.

"I have to go to the can again," Sam said. "And I don't want to miss nothin'."

He got to his feet (*creak, creak*) and headed for the door, in rather a hurry.

"I'm going, too, Sam," said Tess, breathily.

"I'd rather do it alone, Tess," Sam said, halting for a moment and giving her a look of deeply muted understanding. "But thanks, anyway."

He swung around and headed out of the door. Fast.

"The cook," said Dora.

Dick Charleston, attentive husband (who's the heiress in the family?) looked up from where he was still kneeling. He knew he would have to make the effort to get to his feet again before long, but he was hoping that if he put it off as long as possible, maybe his knees would sort of soften up or something.

"What's that, darling?" he said.

"The cook," Dora replied. "Isn't it obvious the cook murdered him? The butler is dead; all the rest of us were in this room except her. No one else could get in or out of the house. So that only leaves the cook."

Dick may have been impressed by this icy feminine logic, but someone else was not.

Sidney Wang jumped to his feet. *Crack. Crack.* A brief look of pain passed across his inscrutable Chinese face, especially when the left knee went. But he bravely ignored it.

"Blade eight inches long," he told Dora. "As you

149

see, it is up to hilt. Would take enormous power to strike such blow. Woman not capable of such power."

Jessie Marbles got to her feet, in the process somewhat resembling an elephant rising from a respectful kneeling position in front of some maharajah or other. Or maybe Queen Victoria. Plus two knee-cracks that sounded like a couple of cannons being fired off by way of salute.

She looked at Wang, eye to eye.

"A woman not capable of a blow of such power, but a man would be, eh?" she said. "Do I take your point?"

"Exactly," said Sidney Wang.

Jessie Marbles drew herself up.

"Are you a chauvinist, Mr. Wang?"

"Certainly not, you silly woman," Sidney Wang retorted.

It looked as if war was about to break out again between the assembled sleuths. Jessie Marbles would have drawn herself up for a crushing retort, only she was drawn up already. Hastily she began the process of drawing herself down, ready to draw herself up once more.

And then, she thought, what a crushing retort there'll be. Something to do with the well-known inability of the Chinese race to . . . to . . . to . . . Hell, there must be a well-known inability of the Chinese race to do *something*. Something that will make this Oriental ostrich look good and unvirile. Yes, those would be the lines to go on. Lack of virility. Hit 'em where it hurts most. Something like this. Let me see. "Silly woman I may be, Mr. Wang, but . . ." But . . . but . . . Dammit, there must be something.

Mercifully her dilemma was solved for her.

The door just behind the prostrate corpse of Lionel Twain was suddenly thrust open, and a voice made itself heard. A voice coming from between tight lips.

"The cook didn't do it, that's for sure."

They all turned to look at Sam Diamond standing in the open doorway. Behind his back he was holding something.

"What makes you certain of this, Diamond?" Milo Perrier asked.

Sam looked at him coolly.

"To drive a knife that far up a man's back," he answered, "you'd need a powerful right arm. Right?"

"Correct," Milo Perrier agreed.

Sam's face remained coolly confident.

"Well," he said slowly, "this arm don't look that strong to me." And from behind his back he whipped the right arm of a woman, up to the elbow.

Dora and Tess screamed.

Again. But isn't that what women are for? To provide a few good noisy screams at moments of sudden excitement.

"Is . . ." said Dora, her voice quivering. "Is that the cook's arm?"

"It ain't the pussycat's tail, lady," Sam answered laconically and through tight lips.

He gave her a grin.

"Oh, don't be alarmed," he went on. "It ain't real. For that matter, neither is the cook."

"The cook?" said Milo Perrier.

"Not real?" said Sidney Wang.

"The cook not real?" said Dick Charleston.

"Not real? The cook?" said Jessie Marbles.

"No," Sam said, "not real."

He turned and reached back into the hall, grasped hold of something, and pulled. There was a grinding, slithering noise. Into everyone's view slid a huge carrying case, the sort of thing in which a musical instrument, a large musical instrument, might be taken from place to place.

Sam dragged it to a convenient space just past the knife-stuck body of the late Lionel Twain.

As he grunted and heaved his way to his chosen spot he explained.

"I found the arm (*grunt*) on the floor. The index (*puff*) finger was pointing (*grunt*) to one of the doors out (*puff, puff*) there. So I went and (*grunt*) opened the (*puff*) door, and (*grunt, grunt, grunt*) found this."

With a sudden swift gesture he unsnapped the lock of the big carrying case. Its lid sprang open. The other

151

sleuths crowded around, pushing and elbowing. Their companions did their best to get a look in over their shoulders.

In the case, laid out with the utmost neatness, were the bits of the cook.

They looked as if they were indeed the dismembered parts of a real human being, except that where they should have joined together there were no sectioned views of lots of bone, sinews, veins, arteries, and other assorted human insides. Instead there were only neat flesh-colored blanks. But all the parts were there, each in its custom-built styrofoam pocket. Two feet, small feminine. Two calves, pretty and well rounded. Two thighs, ditto. One middle section (pass over quickly). One trunk, complete with two (pass over quickly). One lower left arm, and a vacant pocket. Two upper arms, well rounded. One head, vacant expression.

"A mannequin!" exclaimed Milo Perrier, quick as light.

"A mannequin, a robot, a dummy, whatever you call it," Sam said. "Perfect to the last detail with the exception of being able to make her hear or speak."

He turned away and looked down at the prostrate corpse of the late Lionel Twain.

"My hat's off to that guy with the shiv up his back," he said. "Except for the fact that he's dead, he was no dope."

"Nice going, Sam," Tess said, acknowledging the neatness of the impromptu epitaph.

Sam smiled at her, sadly.

"The can is empty now, sweetheart," he said. "But I'd wait a couple of minutes."

Dick Charleston was still contemplating the big carrying case.

"A charming woman," he commented. "A woman of parts."

If Sam was going in for the impromptu epitaph business, surely it was up to a man of more—well, of more, shall we say, polish, to go one better.

He puffed out his chest with modest pride.

His wife interrupted.

Wives.

152

And she the one with the purse strings, too.

She gave a little cough.

"I hope you all realize," she said, "that someone in this room is a murderer?"

Nobody seemed to feel much like saying, "Why, yes, that's so. But everyone plainly was thinking of it. If Lionel Twain had been murdered and both the two members of his staff were accounted for, one having been seen to be dead as well and the other being currently on show in a thoroughly dismembered state, then, since the house was barred, bolted, and shuttered on time locks, one of those present in the dining room at that moment must be the one who had stuck the long, keen-bladed butcher's knife into Lionel Twain's back. Up to the hilt.

Logic. Even if it had been a woman who had stated the case.

So who could it be, this murderer?

One of the five sleuths themselves? Say, Sidney Wang? Or Milo Perrier? Or Sam Diamond? Or, since elderly though she is there can be no doubt that the formidable old detective from the village of Mead St. Mary, Sussex, England, is a pretty tough cookie, could it be Miss Jessica Marbles? Or—but this was a thought that with true feminine logic Dora Charleston did not let enter her pretty little head—could it be Dick Charleston?

But perhaps none of the detectives had turned murderer. Then the guilty one must be one of the five people they had brought with them. Their five trusted associates.

Was it Sidney Wang's Number Three adopted son, Willie? Or Milo Perrier's inseparable chauffeur-cum-*secrétaire,* Marcel Cassette? Or Tess Skeffington (she's been around), secretary and mistress of Sam Diamond? Or how about, since it's a good old rule in these matters always to look for the least likely person, how about Nurse Withers? And, though with true feminine logic this was not a thought Dora Charleston had let enter her pretty little head, could it be Dora Charleston?

Well, in logic, it could.

153

But no one cared to muse aloud on any one of these little logical trains of thought.

So instead Jessie Marbles directed a baleful glance back down at the corpse.

"Interesting," she said thoughtfully. "Twain said he would be stabbed in the back eleven or twelve times. And there they are—eleven or twelve wounds."

"I'm glad I didn't get any dinner," Dora said faintly. "I'd throw up."

Sidney Wang looked all round.

"For sake of ladies present," he said, "may I suggest we all return to drawing room? My son will cover up remains of Mr. Twain."

"Why me, Pop?" Willie demanded indignantly.

"Because you not my real son anyway," Sidney Wang answered, with inexorable Chinese chop-logic.

He turned to the others.

"Come, please."

One by one they filed out, leaving poor downtrodden Willie to perform the gruesome task of covering up the eleven- or twelve-times-punctured corpse of the man who had invited them to dinner, and a murder, the late Lionel Twain.

Whom, if logic is anything, one of them must have murdered.

But which one?

17

In the drawing room of the big old house, with its curious array of objects on the walls, those grim reminders of the nasty things people did to each other in the good old times, and that death's head over the mantelpiece that had seemed to howl aloud its agonies, the nine of them looked at each other in uneasy silence.

The same thought must have been in each head. "Which of us is it?" In every head but one. The head that knows.

But the silence did not last for long. Willie Wang broke it. He came in with a smile on his face that was so bouncingly cheerful no one could have failed to notice it. He closed the door carefully but in haste, as if he could not wait to perform the little task before turning to something far more important.

"I covered him up, Pop," he announced loudly.

And then he added what it was at once obvious he had been longing to come out with all along.

"I wonder how you missed it, Pop," he said.

"Missed what?" Sidney Wang jabbed out, abruptly alarmed.

Willie gave a broad smile, luxuriating in whatever thought was in his head.

"The world's five greatest living detectives," he drawled, "and not one of you noticed that in his hand the late Lionel Twain was clutching . . . this."

And with a flourish he produced from his own

clenched hand a small piece of carefully folded white paper. A note. A note from the murder victim's own body.

"Give it to me," thundered Sidney Wang, in a voice which has scared the living daylights out of three hundred and eighty-six murderers at the last count. "Give it to me."

"No," Willie jabbed back. "I found it."

"Hand it over."

"No, it's mine."

"Give it to me, I say."

"Finders keepers, so yah."

"Give it to me."

It might have gone on forever. Only Milo Perrier decided to step in, with the full weight of his authority.

"Give it to your father," he said commandingly. "You young idiot."

"Idiot? We'll see who's the idiot, *Monsieur* Perrier."

The full weight of Milo Perrier's authority seemed to be a little on the light side.

Willie looked even more cocksure than before.

"The million dollars Twain offered goes to the one who solves the crime," he said. "And that could be me just as well as any of you detectives. I've got more brains than my father gives me credit for. Number Three adopted son! I'm sick and tired of being Number Three adopted son."

He puffed out his chest as full as it would go.

"I'm Willie Wang," he said. "Willie Wang, Young Detective, and this clue—"

He held the folded paper up tauntingly.

"—this clue belongs to me, and no one's going to get it from me. Understand?"

Click.

He whirled round.

Sam Diamond was standing behind him. The click he had heard had come from Sam's gun. It was being held right up close to his ear.

Sam waited till he saw that young Willie had fully registered the situation. And then he spoke not to the boy but to Tess.

"Move away from where you're standing," he told

her. "I don't want you to get hurt when the bullet comes outta his other ear."

Willie gulped and held out the note for Sam to take. Enough said.

Sam put the gun back in his shoulder holster and unfolded the note. He read it aloud.

"Please call Dairy Maid and stop delivery on milk— Lionel Twain, deceased."

He directed a scathing look at Willie.

"So much for your clue, kid."

Willie turned to his father with a sheepish smile.

"Sorry, Dad," he said. "Maybe we could have dinner tomorrow and talk things over, hey, Pop?"

"Hope you like trip back to Yokohama," Sidney Wang said with inscrutable Oriental grimness.

But Milo Perrier was bored with this family bickering.

"Ladies and gentlemen," he said, "I suggest we get down to—'ow you say—business and sort out the— 'ow you say—facts. It is now . . ."

He pulled his watch out of his pocket.

"It is now 12:30 a.m., Sunday morning. The doors and windows of this locked house will automatically open at dawn. And then one of us will be one million— 'ow you say—dollars the richer."

He paused, looking around from face to face.

"And one of us," he added grimly, "will be going to the gas chamber to be hung."

"One, *Monsieur* Perrier?" Jessie Marbles quickly questioned.

She gave a contemptuous snort.

"One?" she repeated. "Why not two? We all have associates."

"Why not four or six or eight?" Sam Diamond put in, rapidly joining the numbers game. "I don't trust none of youse. Maybe I'm just the patsy being set up to take the fall. But I'm not falling for anyone, understand?"

"Not even me, Sam?" Tess said, eyelashes working overtime.

Sam rounded on her.

"Why don't you fall in love with the Jap kid and get off my back?" he snarled, through tight lips.

He turned angrily away and lit a cigarette.

But now Sidney Wang was bored with the marital— or what have you bickering.

"Can we get back to case, please?" he demanded. "It's getting very late and my eyes are getting tired."

"I thought they always looked like that," said a voice through tight lips.

"Knock it off, Sam," Jessie Marbles put in, adopting an American idiom for her American friend.

Sam turned.

"Sorry," he said. "This case is getting on my nerves."

He grinned ruefully at Wang.

"I apologize, fatso."

"Thank you," said Sidney Wang, with grave Oriental dignity.

"Now then," he added with Oriental briskness, "facts, please. Mr. Twain predicts murder and predicts victim to be at dining table. Correct?"

"Correct," said Dora Charleston.

"Sorry, darling," her husband put in, mindful of questions of status, "but this is strictly official."

He turned to Wang.

"Correct," he said.

Wang continued his analysis.

"Twain also predicts murder to take place at midnight and predicts number of stab wounds. Correct?"

"Corr—" said Dora.

"Correct," said Dick.

Wang resumed.

"How can these predictions be so, if Twain is not indeed in collaboration with murderer?"

Milo Perrier stepped forward. If they were on to the logical analysis part, he had been logically analyzing since the year dot.

"If you are implying," he said, not without a trace of huffiness, "that Twain hired one of us to do it you are—'ow you say?—mistaken, Mr. Wang."

He looked around to make sure he had everyone's full attention. A Perrier analysis was not something to be heard with only half an ear.

158

"Supposing for argument's sake," he resumed, "that it was I, Milo Perrier, that Twain hired as his accomplice. At midnight, I would reveal that I was the—'ow you say?—murderer, thereby solving the crime and thus becoming entitled to the—'ow you say?—one million dollars. And at the same time I would prove that I, Milo Perrier, was the Number One Detective, and not Twain."

A quick check to see that everyone was following this brilliant train of deductive thinking, and he continued.

"So Twain would get nothing out of it all, and I would, of course, find a brilliant way to escape to a quiet beach in Rio where there would be an assured supply of hot chocolate."

He shook his head sadly.

"No," he concluded, "I think the accomplice theory does not hold—'ow you say?—water, *Monsieur* Wang."

"Speaking of holding water," Sam Diamond said urgently, "will you all excuse me again?"

"Just a few minutes more, Mr. Diamond," Wang said. "Then we can all retire for the evening."

Sam's battered face took on an expression of grim endurance.

"Go on," he said, crossing his legs.

Dick Charleston took up the hunt.

"What if Twain did it himself?" he proposed.

"Himself?" queried Jessie Marbles. "Murdered himself? For what possible reason? And, come to that, how?"

"The motive is simple," Dick answered. "Ego."

Ego. His listeners considered it. And since they were all pretty powerful egoists themselves, it took a good deal of considering.

Dick waited a little and then went on.

"If we were not to solve this crime," he said, "Twain would indeed be named the world's foremost detective. With an ego like his, the fact that he had to die for it would be a small price to pay."

He looked around. It seemed that he was holding his audience, even convincing them.

He went on yet more eagerly.

"As to how, any man who can create this chamber of electronic marvels could certainly devise a machine that could stab himself in the back eleven or twelve times. *N'est-ce pas?*"

"No, thank you," Perrier said, for once not feeling the need for hot chocolate, neither Nestlé's nor Hershey's nor Cadbury's nor anyone else's.

Dora looked up at her husband with wide eyes.

"That was wonderful, darling," she said.

As far as she was concerned the case was closed, the murder solved.

"Let's go to bed," she said.

She gave her husband another admiring look and added just one word.

"Quickly."

"One moment, please," said Sidney Wang, oblivious of this husband-wife relationship.

"One moment, please. Very interesting theory, Mr. Charleston, but you overlook one very important point."

"And that is?" Dick asked, considerably nettled (and not only by anyone questioning his theory).

Wang looked at him with grave Oriental courtesy.

"It's stupid," he said. "It's the most stupid theory I have ever heard."

"Do you have a better one?" Dick challenged him, the thought of that bed still much in his mind.

"Yes," Wang said, "much better."

He looked around to make sure that he, in his turn, had got the full attention of every single person present, Nurse Withers, still gently snoring, not counting as a person.

Assured that he had total attention, he answered Dick's question.

"Yes, I have a better theory, Mr. Charleston. I did my homework. For example . . ."

He lifted his eyes to the ceiling and pretended to select a single item from among many—the cunning old Oriental—and then, when his audience's attention was just on the point of slipping away, he produced it.

"For example, I have information, Mr. Charleston, that your wife's portfolio of stocks was depleted in

160

latest financial crisis. In short, Mr. Charleston, you are flat broke. You have been borrowing money for over two years . . ."

He paused before delivering the punch line.

"You have been borrowing money for over two years—at seventeen percent interest—from Mr. Lionel Twain."

Pretty good punch line. Big reaction from audience. Gasps. Looks of horror. Swift exchanged glances.

And from Dora Charleston something a bit stronger.

"Broke?" she exclaimed.

"Dickie?" she exclaimed.

"It this true?" she exclaimed.

Dick swallowed. He attempted a smile. It was not a very good attempt. So he swallowed again. Which seemed easier.

"I didn't want to tell you, darling," he managed to say at last. "I was saving it for your birthday."

"One million dollars," said Sidney Wang inexorably, "would buy a great many tight suits, would they not, Mr. Charleston?"

"See here, Wang"—Dick began.

But he was interrupted.

By Dora.

"Dead broke, Dickie?" she exclaimed.

"Almost, darling," he replied, again attempting a smile. "I've got a dollar seventeen."

Dora did not look mollified.

"And some stamps," Dick added hastily.

Stamps did not seem to appease Dora, either. Dick swallowed. Smiles were just not available any more.

"But," he said urgently to her, "I did not murder Lionel Twain."

She did not look altogether trusting.

"You do believe that, Dora?" he asked. "Don't you, Dora?"

"Dora?"

"We'll talk," Dora said. "We'll see."

She turned away. It looked as though one hell of a lot of talking would have to be done before Dick and Dora Charleston climbed into the conjugal bed that night.

161

Dick addressed the others. There were beads of sweat on his elegant forehead.

"It could have been any of you," he said hotly. "Since the discovery of the butler's body, each and every one of us detectives was out of the dining room at one time or another. There would have been ample opportunity for any one of us to commit the crime. Not just me. Not just me."

A circle of implacable faces regarded him. He was on the hot spot, and no one looked the least inclined to get him off it.

He licked his lips and went on, desperately.

"As for motives, there may be more than ego or cash involved. There may be, for instance, revenge."

He took a slow look around at the ring of faces watching him. Had one of them winced, almost imperceptibly, at the mention of the word "revenge"? Was there one who had, after all, suffered somehow at the hands of Lionel Twain and might want to take his revenge? Or her revenge?

But the ring of faces remained locked. If that word had struck home anywhere, the wounded heart had not betrayed itself.

"Revenge?" said Sidney Wang. "Meaning what, Mr. Charleston?"

"Meaning," Dick replied, his voice gradually regaining confidence, "that I am not the only one here who had had a past experience with Mr. Twain. For one thing, did you know that he was quite a ladies' man in his day?"

He looked around the circle of faces once more. Did his glance linger a little longer on one rather than on any of the others? Was there somebody who knew to his cost that Lionel Twain, little pink-tuxedoed dandy, had been in his day quite a ladies' man?

But there was no way of telling. The circle was silent. Until Milo Perrier stepped a little forward.

"Are you suggesting," he said, "that someone here—"

Dick cut across his question and completed it.

"—was at one time in love with Mr. Lionel Twain.

162

Yes, I am suggesting just that. I am more than suggesting it. I am telling it to you as a fact."

He paused, poised to strike. Did anyone, even now, betray that they might have something to fear? They did not.

Dick Charles delivered his blow.

"I am telling you as a fact," he said "that Lionel Twain was once engaged to, and jilted, Miss Jessica Marbles."

Jessica Marbles's face now betrayed all. However Dick had unearthed the facts, it seemed he had hit on the truth, or enough of the truth to have shaken even the formidable tweed-clad form of Jessie Marbles.

"Mon—'ow you say—*dieu!"* exclaimed Milo Perrier.

So violent was the exclamation it actually woke Nurse Withers.

"Jesus H Christ!" she exclaimed.

And dropped off to sleep again.

Dick Charleston's eyes were blazing with triumph.

"Yes," he said, "jilted at the altar fifty-four years ago. Left in that same baggy tweed outfit she's wearing now."

"How do you know this?" Sidney Wang asked.

"I subscribe," Dick answered, his voice ringing in victory, "to old copies of the London *Times*. All information is eventually valuable."

"Is this true, Jess?" asked her old buddy-buddy Sam Diamond.

Jessie Marbles sniffed. Loudly.

"I was not jilted," she declared. "I walked out on *him*. He wanted to fool around before the wedding."

Milo Perrier, gallant to the last, came to her aid.

"And being the lady you are," he suggested, "you refused?"

"Not completely," Jessica Marbles answered. "But it got out of hand. He wanted me to say nasty words. The man was horrid. I could have killed him then."

Glances flashed from face to face.

"But," Jessie Marbles added, "I got over it—about two weeks ago."

"That's good enough for me," said old buddy-buddy Sam, through tight lips.

163

He turned to Milo Perrier.

"How about you, Frenchie?"

"I am not a Frenchie," Milo Perrier retorted, reddening like a little turkeycock with undiluted rage. "I'm a Belgy!"

He subsided a little.

"And as for other motives for this atrocious crime," he added on a more somber note, "how about patricide?"

"The killing of one's own parent," Dick Charleston quickly explained for the benefit of anyone who might not know the meaning of the word.

He looked with interest at the little Belgy detective.

"You mean," he asked, "that Lionel Twain was the father of someone in this room?"

Glances of suspicion darted from one to another. The cat had been put among the pigeons again, and with a vengeance.

Would someone crack? Would a guilty secret force words from reluctant lips?

It would.

Tess Skeffington spoke.

"He—" she said. "He—"

She made a tremendous effort.

"Lionel Twain wasn't my father," she brought out at last. "He was my uncle."

"He . . . he . . . he was very good to me. He would take me to the circus. And give me candy."

She sobbed again at the recollection of that candy.

"We—" she stammered out. "we stopped going when I was about twenty-six."

She turned a tear-stained face toward the battered figure of Sam Diamond.

"I'm sorry, Sam," she wailed.

"Twenty-six?" Sam retorted. "Twenty-six? What the hell kind of circus was it?"

But he got no answer.

Milo Perrier had stopped another pace forward.

"Forgive me," he interrupted, "but I was talking about patricide, not uncle-cide."

He sounded hurt and annoyed. But then who wouldn't if they had started a discussion on patricide

164

only to find they had been sidetracked into a discussion on uncle-cide.

He breathed fiercely down his nose.

"Lionel Twain," he said to Tess, "may have been your uncle. But he was not your father. He was, in fact, the illegitimate—'ow you say—father of *Monsieur* Sidney Wang."

Every face turned to Sidney Wang.

Sidney Wang maintained his look of inscrutable Oriental impassivity.

"Not true," he countered. "Not true that Lionel Twain was illegitimate father. I was adopted. I have my papers. That is why I have adopted all my children."

"Yeah," Willie Wang murmured. "I was kinda wondering . . ."

His adopted father went on.

"Lionel Twain loved me very much. But when I was nineteen, one day he called me into his study . . ."

His voice trailed away as the recollected scene came back to his memory. The old study. The father's call.

"He called me into his study and happened to notice I was Oriental. He kicked me out of the house. I could have—"

He checked himself.

Too late.

Milo Perrier completed the telltale, giveaway sentence.

"Have killed him. Eh, *Monsieur* Wang? You could have—'ow you say—killed him, isn't it? Yes? Yes? *Oui? Oui?*"

"Stop," Sam Diamond yelled suddenly.

All eyes turned to him.

An expression of intense pain was on his battered face.

"Didn't I tell you I needed the can?" he burst out. "Wee, wee. How could you do that to me?"

Sidney Wang ignored the outburst.

"Yes, *Monsieur* Perrier," he said, "I could have killed Lionel Twain—as easily as you. Because Lionel Twain killed only thing you ever loved. Marie-Louise Cartier."

"Your sweetheart?" Dick asked, a sudden wave of

165

sympathy coming over him for this pudgy little man who once had loved and loved deeply.

"My poodle," replied Milo Perrier.

A look of infinite sorrow spread over his egg-shaped face.

"Lionel Twain was a cruel man," he told them. "Every—'ow you say—fall—"

"Autumn, man, autumn," Jessie Marbles interrupted him. "Remember you're British."

She looked at him with scorn.

"Even if you're not."

Rebuked, Milo Perrier took up his tale.

"Every year around September Lionel Twain would come to—'ow you say—Belgium to hunt zee poodle."

He gave a sob.

"The day they brought her bloodied sequin collar to me," he muttered, "I vowed that one day I would—"

"Knock him off?" suggested Sam Diamond.

"Yes," Milo Perrier admitted. "Yes, if I had the chance, gladly. But I did not have that—'ow you say—chance. Somebody here beat me to it."

"So," said Sam thoughtfully "there was more than one reason we were invited here. Not only was Twain testing our skills as detectives, but we all had a legitimate motive for doing the old man in."

"Have not heard your motive yet, Mr. Diamond," Sidney Wang reminded him.

Sam smiled sadly.

"The motive wasn't important," he said. "Let's just put it I hated him enough to kill him."

"You are a closed man, Mr. Diamond," Wang said. "You hide many things. Could it be that Mr. Twain found out your secret?"

Sam stiffened.

"I don't know what you're talking about," he said, through tight lips.

Sidney Wang wheeled around to face Tess.

"Doesn't he, Miss Skeffington?" he asked shrewdly.

Every one of them looked at Tess. She lowered her eyes.

"Twain picked Sam up at a gay bar," she murmured.

"I was workin' in a case," Sam snapped. "Woikin'."

166

"Every night?" Tess asked. "For six months?"

"I got fifty bucks a day expenses," he defended himself. "I hate them queeries."

"Twain had Polaroid pictures of Sam in drag," Tess told them sadly.

"I was in disguise," Sam shouted. "Disguise, dammit. Lotsa dames go in them joints. I never kissed nobody, and I never did nothin' to a man that I wouldn't do with a woman. And . . . and . . . and I didn't kill Twain."

His voice had risen to a ringing shout. Then, suddenly, it dropped. He turned to Tess and spoke softly, almost lovingly.

"Bitch."

"Interesting," commented Sidney Wang. "All have perfect motives for killing Mr. Twain. Most interesting."

Jessie Marbles puffed out a sigh like a dying whale.

"We still have the night to get through," she said. "If anyone is to solve this case, I say we get a good night's sleep."

"An admirable suggestion," Milo Perrier came smoothly in. "And an even better one is to lock your doors. One of us is—'ow you say—ruthless."

And on that happy note the five sleuths and their five associates made their way to beddy-bye-byes.

And to sleep?

18

The big old house on Lola Lane lay silent in the darkness. In the cold and deserted kitchen not a mouse stirred. The only mouse the house had known had been the one carefully introduced into the bedroom given to the Charlestons in the hope that one or the other of them would discover it shortly after the secret of the baking flour dust and the sugary cobwebs had been found out.

In the empty dining room the soup plates and the cutlery lay on the long table, sole remains of the meal that had never been eaten. In the gruesome drawing room all was now still. In an ashtray lay the butts of Sam Diamond's cigarettes.

The high hallway with its suits of old armor and its animals' heads was quiet, too. Not a whisper disturbed it. The library, with its rank on rank of mystery novels bound in rare old calf, was equally deserted and equally silent. Even the smoldering fire seemed to have quietly extinguished itself.

On the floor above, where the five bedrooms allocated to the five sleuths lay, all seemed to be quiet, too. Along the drafty corridor only drafts whistled.

And up above that? What about the concealed chamber at the very top of the house where there is a battery of TV monitors? Is there anyone there now to see the pictures that flicker on those screens?

Pictures do flicker there. That much is certain. There is a row of five screens, each one connected to a secret camera which keeps a watchful and baleful eye on each of the five occupied bedrooms on the floor below. And, though all seems quiet in those rooms, on each of the screens there is something to see. On each of the loudspeakers connected to bugging microphones in those rooms there is something to hear.

In the bedroom that was allocated to the Wangs, there could be observed two recumbent shapes in the bed that still looked the worse for the fire Benson had lit in it. The Wangs, father and son, seemed to be asleep, both wearing their hats. The massive bolt on the door could be seen to have been vigorously snicked into place. All might seem to be tranquil.

But in the semidarkness Willie Wang's tirelessly optimistic voice suddenly rose.

"What do you think, Pop?"

"I wonder . . ." replied Sidney Wang.

"Yes?" said Willie, all bright hope.

"Why you sleep with shoes on."

"In case we're attacked in the middle of the night, Pop," Willie replied.

A silence followed. Any watcher on that TV monitor could almost have heard Willie striving not to ask his next question. But the silence was not very long.

"Pop, who do you think is the murderer?"

"Must sleep on it," Sidney Wang replied. "Will know in morning when I wake up."

"What if you don't wake up, Pop?"

"Then *you* did it," Wang replied, unanswerably.

But, just to make sure, he added a fatherly admonition.

"Go to sleep. Now."

"Yes, Pop. Good night, Pop."

Willie planted a son-like kiss on his father's fatherlike cheek.

"Should have adopted a dog," Sidney Wang said sadly.

He heaved himself over and pulled the covers around his ears.

Silence followed.

It was not very long.

The room was suddenly filled with a harsh "Sssssss" of sound.

"Should I turn off the steam-heating, Pop?" the unwearying Willie asked.

Sidney Wang gave no reply.

The "Sssssss" grew louder and harsher.

"Pop?"

"Ssssssssss"

"Pop?"

Willie's voice grew louder and harsher.

"Pop?"

"Is not steam," came the voice of Sidney Wang from the borders of sleep. "Someone just put deadly snake into room. Wake up father when it comes near bed."

Up in the viewing room above, another of the monitor screens abruptly showed signs of life. It was the one connected to the bedroom allocated to the Charlestons.

"I want you to know something, Dickie darling," the voice of Dora came over the bugging microphone.

A silence followed while Dickie waited to hear what she wanted him to know.

Dora's voice came again.

"I want you to know that if you're the murderer, I still love you."

Pause. Dickie waited to gather the consequence of this statement.

Dora's voice floated up again.

"I don't think it would be right to make love, but I still love you."

There was a long pause while Dick considered this. Any watcher up in the viewing room would have been somewhat disappointed.

"Well, let's see what we have here," Dick said at last.

"We have one missing dead naked butler."

He ticked the dead missing naked butler off on the fingers of his hand.

"We have one host with butcher's knife in his back."

He ticked off one host on the next finger.

"We have one dismembered electronic mute cook."

171

He ticked off the dismembered electronic mute cook on the next finger.

"And," he said, "we have one deadly poisonous scorpion crawling up our sheets."

He ticked off the deadly poisonous scorpion on the next finger.

"Is that what that is?" Dora asked. "I've been wondering."

"Oh, yes," Dickie reassured her. "They can kill instantly. I suggest we don't move, darling."

"For how long?"

"Quite possibly, the rest of our lives."

All was still once more in the Charlestons' bedroom. Deathly still.

The screen showing events in the bedroom which had been given to Miss Jessie Marbles and her faithful nurse, Miss Withers, showed the two old dears in bed with their tasseled nightcaps on their dear old heads. The voice of Miss Marbles boomed suddenly out in the semidarkness like a ship's foghorn plaintively bleating in some desolate and treacherous sea.

"Are you sleeping, Nurse?"

Silence.

Not even the hiss of a deadly snake nor the patter of tiny scorpion feet disturbed the calm.

"I said, are you sleeping?"

But the silence persisted deeper than that, freezing Willie Wang into terror-stricken dumbness as the venom-tongued snake slid inch by inch across the floor toward the bed where he lay beside his venerable and, dammit, sleeping father. Deeper, too, than the silence enfolding Dick and Dora Charleston as, tipetty-tip, tipetty-tip, the scorpion scrambled its way along the sheets thinking about a midnight snack.

"Nurse, are you dead?"

The foghorn voice bellowed.

"No."

"Then say so," Jessie Marbles fumed. "It's really *very* annoying not to know."

Remark received in blank silence.

"Now be quiet," Jessie Marbles went fiercely on, "and just let me think."

Nurse Withers was quiet, bar a faint zizzing sound. Miss Marbles thought, faint whirring sound.

"Hmm," she said after some ten minutes.

Silence once more. No hiss of snake, no pitter-patter of scorpion.

Ten more minutes passed.

"Yes . . ." said Miss Marbles with some satisfaction.

Silence. The whirr of brain, the zizz of snore.

"Yes . . ."

A trace more self-satisfied this time.

Then silence again.

"Quite possibly."

Very complacent that.

More silence.

". . . and then again . . ."

Pretty complacent that, too. But more silence followed. It was broken by something that sounded like a minor detonation of explosives. Miss Marbles sat up in bed, one and a half inches.

"Good heavens!" she said. "I know who the murderer is."

"Solvey-poo?" asked a voice that had just ceased to zizz.

"Yes, Miss Withers," Jessie Marbles replied triumphantly. "Solvey-poo indeed. The murderer is—"

Suddenly she stopped.

"Good God!" she said. "Gas."

"I'm sorry," said Nurse Withers. "I can't help it. I'm old."

"No, no," Jessie Marbles replied roughly. "The *other* kind of gas. The kind that kills."

"Sometimes my gas . . ." Nurse Withers murmured apologetically.

But Miss Marbles had left her bed. It was a process that somewhat resembled an elephant leaving the jungle in a deuce of a hurry owing to the unexpected presence of the Jungle Boy, or Mr. Rudyard Kipling or Mr. Walt Disney. She went hunting around the room, sniffing like a demented whale.

"It's seeping in through the vent," she boomed at last.

She strode over to the door and seized the handle. The door resisted, massively.

"Locked from the outside," pronounced Miss Marbles.

A fit of coughing seized her, much in the way the Empire State Building might be rocked in a minor earthquake.

"The windows," she exclaimed.

She rushed over and flung back the heavy velvet drapes. Blank steel shutters confronted her.

"Locked," she cried. A percipient detective, Miss Jessica Marbles.

"Help!" she cried.

A lady in distress, Miss Jessica Marbles.

From the bed came a faint and supercilious sniff.

"Doesn't smell that bad to me," Nurse Withers grumbled.

If things were happening in Miss Marbles's room, they were beginning to happen on one of the other TV monitors up above, too. Tess was in bed while Sam was pacing the floor, smoking.

"Did I do right, Sam?" Tess said abruptly. "Telling them about the gay bar?"

"Perfect, sweetheart," Sam replied, through tight lips. "They took the bait like dumb halibut."

He smiled, grimly.

"Let them think I'm a pansy," he said. "While they're busy suspecting me, one of them is going to let his pants down."

Tess considered that in silence for a little. Then she asked another question.

"Sam, why do you keep all those naked muscle men magazines in your office?"

"Suspects," Sam Diamond snapped back, quick as a whip. "Always lookin' for suspects."

He stopped his pacing with dramatic suddenness, whirled around, and looked hard at the foot of the locked door.

"Hello," he said, "someone just shoved a note under."

With a few quick strides he went over. He stopped. He picked up the note, opened it, and read.

"Now that you're locked in tight from both sides,

Mr. Diamond, I know you'll be glad to know there's a bomb ticking away in your clock. It will go off if you just look at it. Signed, da murderer."

He turned and looked hard at Tess.

"Sorry about this," he said. "And me owin' you all that money, too."

Tess looked at him with blinking eyes.

"That's all right, Sam," she said. "But what are we going to do?"

A look of firm decision came onto Sam's rugged features.

"I've got an idea," he said, through tight lips. "I don't know if it's gonna work or not."

His eyes flashed from point to point in the room.

"Quick," he said, through tight lips. "Turn your back."

Obediently Tess humped around in the bed.

"Whatever you do," Sam warned her, "don't turn around."

"I won't, Sam."

"Good. Because I think I'm gonna cry."

In the viewing room above, the sound of Sam Diamond sobbing his little hard heart out like a child, a poor little chee-ild, came ringing over the loudspeaker. But sounds could also be heard on the speaker monitoring the room into which Benson, the butler, had shown Milo Perrier and his faithful chauffeur-cum-*secrétaire*. In the big fourposter double bed, Milo and Marcel lay side by side.

The plaintive voice of Marcel rose up.

"Thank you for letting me sleep in the same bed with you, *monsieur*. I feel much safer."

From out of the semidarkness the voice of Milo Perrier rose up. It sounded cross.

"You may stay in the bed, but you are not to sleep. You will be my bodyguard. In other words, you are to guard my—'ow you say—body."

Into the semidarkness the voice of Marcel rose up. It was very indignant.

"It's your body, you guard it! You only pay me for being a chauffeur."

"A chauffeur-cum-*secrétaire*!!!"

"No, you only pay me for being a chauffeur."

"Very well," said Milo Perrier, with immense dignity. "Then go sleep in the car."

"You are unfair," Marcel replied, with no dignity at all. "I will tell everyone you wear a toupée."

"They already know."

Very dignified statement in the semidarkness.

"Then why do you wear it?"

Very irritating question in the semidarkness.

"I didn't know," Milo Perrier explained, "that you knew."

"Certainly I know. It's a terrible toupée."

The argument might have gone on forever. But at that moment a tiny scratching noise met the keen ear of the little Belgian detective.

"Quiet," he hissed.

Marcel was quiet. He had not quite perfected his next retort, so he was more than content to have a little time to think.

But he was not going to get it.

"Someone is outside the—'ow you say—door," hissed Milo Perrier.

Marcel did not welcome this piece of news.

"Quickly, get out of bed and see who it is."

Marcel welcomed this even less. But he was Milo Perrier's chauffeur-cum-*secrétaire* (even if only the chauffeur bit was paid) and he knew where his duty lay. Nor could he see how to get out of it.

He heaved off the covers and put his bare feet on the cold floor.

"Hurry," whispered Milo Perrier. "Be quick. 'Ow you say? *Dépêchez-vous*."

Marcel crept in his bare feet across to the door. He grasped the handle. He tried to turn it. He succeeded. He tried to pull open the door. He did not succeed.

"It's locked," he hissed.

"Of course it is locked, imbecile," Milo Perrier hissed back. "Did we not all agree to lock our—'ow you say?—doors?"

"*Oui, monsieur.*"

"Well unlock it, *imbécile*."

Marcel drew back the heavy bolt and turned the door handle again. He pulled at the door. It did not open.

"*Monsieur,* it is locked."

"*Imbéc*—"

"From the outside, *monsieur.*"

Milo Perrier wailed. And then he noticed something. Something *affreusement* odd.

"Marcel," he said, "you look taller to me."

"*Monsieur?*"

"Why do you suddenly look taller to me?" his irate employer demanded.

"I do not understand, *monsieur,*" Marcel replied. "I am not getting taller."

Milo Perrier gave himself furiously to think.

"If you are not getting taller," he said, "there is only one alternative when I am seeing that you are getting taller. And that is this."

"*Monsieur?*"

"The room is getting shorter."

Marcel looked at the room. Milo Perrier looked at the room. And there was no doubt about it. The room was getting shorter.

"*Mon dieu,*" remarked Marcel, in character to the last, "the ceiling is coming down."

He was perfectly right. The ceiling was slowly coming down. A moment later it reached the tops of the posts of the big bed. For an instant or two nothing happened. Was the bed going to keep our heroes from disaster? Of course it wasn't. *Crack. Crack. Crack. Crack.* One by one the four posts failed in their duty.

"What will we do?" howled Marcel.

"I do not know," replied Milo Perrier gravely. "But this much I can tell you. This is exactly how they make —'ow you say?—goose liver pâté."

19

Hard against the tall library windows of the old house beat the rain (electronic). Breaking the silence of the big, high-ceilinged room came from time to time the sharp crack and low following rumble of thunder (electronic). Through the windows over which the heavy draperies had still not been drawn came vivid zigzags of greenish purple lightning (electronic).

In the cone of light falling on the desk a pair of hands hovered over a single sheet of thick paper on which was written, in the blackest of inks and the most individual of handwriting, a list of five names. Five names with, beside each one, the name of an associate.

In the hand was a pen. It dipped down and crossed out with one bold black stroke the first name.

Monsieur Milo Perrier (and Marcel Cassette)

A soft cackle of laughter broke the silence. The pen hovered again, dipped, erased.

Sam Diamond (and Tess Skeffington)

Again a soft cackle of laughter, hardly louder than the noise of the coals settling (electronically) in the grate.

For the third time the pen dipped down and a broad black line was run through a name.

Miss Jessica Marbles (and Nurse Withers)

Soft and snickering was the tiny cackle of laughter that followed. Soft and snickering was the fall of the coals in the grate of the big fireplace.

Then again the pen swooped, and a thick black line was scored.

Mr. Dick Charleston (and Mrs. Dora Charleston)

Soft, snickering, and full of malice was the cackle of laughter that followed.

And then the pen poised for the final obliterating stroke. For a moment it hovered over the last name on the list.

Mr. Sidney Wang (and Willie Wang)

It swooped.

It halted.

A voice had spoken in the darkness, a crisp, incisive voice cutting through the velvety gloom.

"Not so fast, please."

It was the voice of Sidney Wang, master detective. Sidney Wang who, not so many minutes before, had been lying peacefully sleeping in a large (and partly fire-ruined) bed while beside him, wide-eyed and paralyzed with fright and wearing his hat, lay his Number Three adopted son, Willie, and toward them both crept the deadliest of all possible snakes, forked tongue drooling.

"Do not make line through my name," Sidney Wang went on, standing composedly in the doorway. "Cross out 'snake' instead."

Behind his father Willie Wang appeared. Round his neck was a snake, very dead. But it was wrapped so tightly that young Willie's eyes were distinctly bulging.

"Nice shot, Pop," he managed to gasp. "But I sure wish you weren't such a heavy sleeper."

He tugged the snake free, and his eyes ceased to bulge.

But, when his father spoke next, they popped.

"And now," Sidney Wang said, in the same level tone he had used throughout, "and now, if you please, one million dollars, Mr. Bensonmum!"

The man at the desk swung his high-backed chair around in fury. And in the cone of light was revealed as Mr. Bensonmum, otherwise plain old Benson the butler. But he was no longer the dead naked butler. Far from it. He was wearing rather a good tuxedo.

"Very clever of you, Mr. Wang," he said.

"But—" said Willie, who had caught a glimpse of unshaded eyes looking in his direction in a thoroughly disconcerting way.

"Oh, yes," said Bensonmum. "As you can see, I can see."

"So I see," said Wang.

Bensonmum relaxed a little and leaned back in his chair.

"Tell me," he said, "as the only living survivor of my little test, Mr. Wang, how did you deduce it was me?"

Sidney Wang smiled a modest little smile.

"Went back to theory very seldom used today," he explained. "Butler did it."

A look of bitter rage crossed Bensonmum's face.

"I hadn't thought of that," he snarled.

But then he recovered a little and darted a shrewd glance at the Chinese sleuth.

"But how do you explain finding my dead body in the kitchen?" he asked sharply.

"Body made of fine plastic," replied Wang placidly. "Same as mute cook. While we were examining plastic butler, you were murdering Mr. Twain."

Glum bafflement expressed itself on Bensonmum's face.

"You're a very clever little laundry man, Mr. Wang," he conceded, though scarcely in the generous spirit which ought to animate the breast of a butler trained in the good old English sporting manner.

But before Sidney Wang had a chance to acknowledge in a good old Chinese sporting manner that he hadn't done "too badly, what," a new voice broke the quiet of the library.

A voice neither Wang himself nor the mysterious Mr. Bensonmum had ever expected to hear.

"Very clever," it said. "But not quite clever enough."

Wang whirled.

Willie whirled.

Bensonmum did not need to whirl. But he did have to stretch his neck to see around Wang and Willie to find out who it was who was standing in the doorway behind them.

It was Jessica Marbles.

"Very clever," she repeated, "but not quite clever enough. I'll take that one million dollars, Bensonmum, alias Irving Goldman."

"Irving Goldman?" Sidney Wang asked in polite perplexity.

Jessica Marbles swung around like a battleship and reached behind her. She located Nurse Withers's wheelchair with in it none other than Nurse Withers and pushed the whole contraption into the room.

"Irving Goldman," she explained, "was the attorney for the *late* Lionel Twain. Twain died five years ago. His body was recently discovered in Goldman's filing cabinet. Goldman was a hundred thousand dollars in debt when he couldn't pay for his son's bar mitzvah. He was, of course—and this should have been evident to the most incompetent observer—a good Jewish father who would never pay less than the going rate when his little son came of age to have his bar mitzvah."

She paused for breath, but, game as ever, soon plunged on.

"So Goldman did in Twain, and then with his accountant, Marvin Metzner, figured out—as you so quaintly say in this country—that if he was to outwit us all for this weekend, he would win the million dollars and through a 1963 I.R.S.—as you so quaintly call Her Majesty's Commissioners of Inland Revenue in this country—loophole, he would only have to pay a twenty-five percent capital gains tax. Am I correct, Mr. Goldman?"

A look of doubly baffled rage crossed the face of Irving Goldman, alias Bensonmum, alias Benson, alias the dead naked butler.

"Correct, Miss Marbles," he admitted. "Only how did you escape from the poison gas?"

"Quite simple," said Jessie Marbles, with a massive shrug of her massive tweed-clad shoulders. "I covered my mouth and let Miss Withers breathe in all the gas."

"Sicky-poo," commented Miss Withers.

"Yes, dear, I know," Jessie Marbles said to her reassuringly.

She turned to Bensonmum, alias Goldman, and held out a massive paw.

"One million dollars, please," she said.

Goldman, alias Bensonmum, put his hand reluctantly into his pocket.

"I wouldn't if I were you, Goldman," said a crisp, incisive voice from the doorway.

Miss Marbles whirled like a battleship.

Nurse Withers whirled, by manipulating the wheels of her chair.

Sidney Wang whirled, in a practiced manner by now.

Willie Wang whirled—like father, like son.

Irving Goldman did not need to whirl because his high-backed chair was still facing the right direction to spot unexpected arrivals in the doorway. Only, as usual, a great many people were standing between him and them. So he had to stick his neck very far out, something he had at least had a lot of practice at. And when he had it stuck out, who should he see but . . .

Dick Charleston.

And, beside him, though a little to the rear in a properly wifely way, who should there be but . . .

Dora Charleston.

"Or," Dick said in a very debonair manner, "should I not say Mr. Goldman, but Mr. Marvin Metzner?"

Marvin Metzner, alias Irving Goldman, alias Bensonmum, alias Benson, alias the dead naked butler, smiled and nodded in affirmation.

"Very good, Mr. Charleston," he said, "but how did you know?"

"The bill in the dead butler's hand," Dick explained, with becoming nonchalance. "It stated that the entire weekend was catered, remember. Well, only an accountant would hold on to a thing like that."

"Dickie," Dora put in urgently from just behind him, "get the money and let's go, please."

The atmosphere in this place was spooky, and it seemed that Dora, very sensibly, did not wish to spend one minute more in it than she had to.

But she had reckoned without the fact that her husband was a Great Detective. A Great Detective does not just collect the money and go. A Great Detective gives an explanation. A Great Explanation. Miss Dorothy L. Sayers's Lord Peter Wimsey on occasion required some thirty closely printed pages for his explanation, and Dick is not going to settle for grabbing any dollars and running, not even a million of them.

"In a moment, darling," he said.

"Goldman," he began, in the sort of patronizing, explaining voice that had ruined the end of one million detective stories for Lionel Twain, "Goldman was killed last month while skiing. He jumped two hundred feet into a low-flying plane."

He stepped forward and confronted Marvin Metzner, alias Goldman, alias Bensonmum, alias Benson, in triumph.

"Before coming here this evening," he went on, "I checked to find out who ordered the stationery on which the invitations were printed. They gave me the name of Carlotta Penelope Aspromonte."

"Dickie," Dora said urgently.

But as well try to stop an avalanche in full cry down the slopes of Mont Blanc as stop a Great Detective in full Explanation.

A terrible gleam had come into Dick's eye.

"Carlotta Penelope Aspromonte," he chanted. "From San Jose."

"Dickie, please."

Dick threw his head back in triumph.

"There is no Carlotta Penelope Aspromonte in San Jose," he said.

He wagged a finger at them and continued.

"But what do those initials spell, ladies and gentlemen?"

Nobody offered to do any spelling.

"They spell C.P.A.," Dick Charleston told them. "Certified Public Accountant."

"Dickie, I can't wait much longer."

But Dora's husband was too intent on seeing how the Great Explanation was going down to hear a word she said. And he seemed to be getting a pretty good reaction from Marvin Metzner, alias Irving Goldman, alias Bensonmum, alias Benson.

"You have not lost your touch, Mr. Charleston," he admitted ruefully. "But tell me, how did you manage to elude the deadly scorpion?"

"We didn't," Dick told him briefly. "He bit Dora. We have fifteen minutes to get to a doctor."

"Explain later, Dickie," Dora wailed. "Let's go."

"We'll make it, darling," Dick said nonchalantly. "Never fear."

But he did make a gesture toward getting a move on. He held out his hand for the million dollars.

"The prize money, Metzner—"

"—belongs to me," a voice completed his sentence from the open door.

Surprise, surprise.

In the doorway, as Dick whirled, Dora whirled, Willie Wang whirled, Sidney Wang whirled, Jessica Marbles whirled, Nurse Withers opened half an eye, and Marvin Metzner, Certified Public Accountant, craned his neck, stood Milo Perrier and Marcel. They looked a little the worse for wear. Their hats appeared to have been crushed by a gigantic force. Their shoulders were bent as if they had had to resist a gigantic force for a long time. Their knees were buckled as if a gigantic force had been applied to them from above. Milo Perrier stepped forward and with an easy wave of his left hand offered an explanation unasked.

"Marcel," he said, "being one of the world's strongest men, stopped your ceiling from crushing us at four feet five inches."

He winced and rubbed the small of his back.

"It may be months before we are able to straighten up again," he said. "But a million dollars will buy a lot of back braces, eh, Miss Irene Twain, daughter of Lionel."

He got a good reaction.

"What?" exclaimed Dora Charleston.

"What?" exclaimed Dick Charleston.

"What?" exclaimed Jessica Marbles.

"Zzzz," exclaimed Nurse Withers.

185

"What?" exclaimed Sidney Wang.

"What?" exclaimed Willie Wang.

But the figure in the chair exclaimed nothing. Which was perhaps the best reaction of all.

Milo Perrier approached, not without a good deal of swagger, despite the sore back and buckled knees.

"Or," he said, "do you prefer to be called *Rita,* Miss Twain?"

"Rita, if you don't mind," answered, in an attractive falsetto, Rita Twain, alias Marvin Metzner, alias Irving Goldman, alias Bensonmum, alias Benson, alias the dead naked butler.

"But," she added, "how did you know?"

Not that Milo Perrier was not going to tell her, and the world.

He took a deep breath.

"Never underestimate a Frenchman's nose, Miss Twain," he said. "And especially, never underestimate the nose of a—'ow you say?—Belgy. At dinner tonight I smelled your Chanel Number Five. It was you who did away with all of them—Metzner, Goldman, and your father. In fact, if you had your way, you would do away with all men, would you not? Men who had made you ashamed and had made you suffer because you were born with brains, talent, money, everything but that which you most desired—'ow you say?—beauty. It is a statement of fact, Miss—'ow you say? —Twain, that as a man you are barely passable, but as a woman, you are—a dog!"

"That's your opinion, big boy," replied Rita Twain, alias Metzner, alias Goldman, alias Bensonmum, alias Benson.

"Dickie," came a small urgent voice from the rear of the onlookers, "can we go? I'm begining to itch."

"One moment, darling, till we clear this up."

But Milo Perrier did not intend to delay the proceedings.

"If you don't mind," he said, "I will take my money and go. With luck I can still make dinner at Maxim's tonight."

"If I were you, I'd just order a tuna fish sandwich."

Whose could this unexpected voice be? The house

is still electronically bolted and barred, shut up with a time lock till dawn breaks over the hills. All the people in the house are assembled here in this room, with the exception of Sam Diamond and Tess. And Sam and Tess have been foully done to death by a bomb ticking away in the clock in their room, a bomb which would go off if it was so much as merely looked at. So who could this be, standing in the doorway and advising Milo Perrier to make his dinner a tuna fish sandwich?

It was Sam Diamond, accompanied by the lovely Tess, and they had escaped the bomb by means which defied the imagination, of course.

"Yeah," said Sam, "don't bother wid that Maxim's stuff, Perrier, because that million dollars belongs to me."

He advanced into the room and addressed the figure still seated in the high-backed chair through tight lips.

"Ain't that right, *Sam*?"

The figure in the chair gave a long snarl of dismay, through tight lips.

"That's right, folks," explained the last of the five to have escaped a terrible death. "Sam Diamond outsmarted us all. That's him sitting in that high-backed chair there, the real Sam Diamond. My name is Loomis, J. J. Loomis. I'm an actor. I do impressions. I did the Carson Show six times last year . . ."

He was really selling himself. And on he went in a breathless gabble, through tight lips.

"Diamond hired me for the weekend. Oh, by the way, Miss Skeffington is actually Wanda Norman. She sells Tupperware at a downtown department store. We was gonna make a hundred bucks for the night, but seeing as how I put all the pieces together, I figure the million bucks belongs to me. Isn't that right, Wanda?"

"That's right, J. J."

"Diamond hated all of yourse," J. J. Loomis continued, through tight lips. "You were all getting rich and he had that crummy little office down by Frisco Bay. He was out to show youse all who Number One was. Isn't that right, Mr. Diamond?"

All eyes turned to Sam Diamond, alias Rita Twain, alias Marvin Metzner, alias Irving Goldman, alias Bensonmum, alias Benson, alias the dead naked butler.

"Wrong," he said. "That would have been so obvious a child could have guessed it. Wrong. Wrong. Wrong."

The five sleuths and their five associates looked in fury at the man they had just learned was Sam Diamond and who only moments earlier they had believed to be Rita Twain, daughter of Lionel, or Marvin Metzner, Certified Public Accountant, or Irving Goldman, attorney, or Bensonmum, figure of mystery, or Benson, butler, or just honest-to-goodness dead naked butler.

Wrong? How dare he tell them that they were wrong? And how could they be wrong?

For a few seconds the person in the high-backed chair regarded them all steadily and, it was plain, with something like contempt. But at last the explanation came.

"No, my dear colleagues, you are all wrong. What you all seem to overlook is the most simple and direct solution."

The sleuths looked at each other. What was the most simple and direct solution? How could they have overlooked anything? Hadn't they between them covered every conceivable combination of people who could have done the murder?

But the figure in the high-backed chair put a hand to his or her neck and began to fiddle with something there. Then, in a single astonishing gesture, he or she gripped the bottom of a rubber mask fitting closely to his or her fiesh and tore it upward.

To reveal underneath the face of Lionel Twain.

Their genial host looked at them all. He sighed.

"You had all been so clever for so long that you had forgotten how to be humble," he said. "You had forgotten to see the obvious for what it is."

He shook his head.

"Yes," he continued, "you have tricked and fooled your followers for so many years that at last you

188

have succeeded in tricking yourselves. You—all of you—failed, ladies and gentlemen."

He put out a hand and rang the little brass bell on the desk beside him.

It surprised none of the silenced sleuths when Benson appeared, correct down to the last button on his black butler's suit.

Lionel Twain looked at the deflated group. And then his voice took on a new note as he turned to Benson.

"Yes, they failed," he said. "But, dammit, they failed magnificently, didn't they, Benson?"

"They did indeed, sir," Benson chimed in.

Lionel Twain looked at the sleuths once more and shook his head ruefully.

"Damn and blast you all," he said, "you've made me love you all over again. The Great Detectives, God bless 'em every one."

ENJOY YOUR FAVORITE MOVIES
OVER AND OVER AT HOME

THE TOWER by Richard Martin Stern   **(59-434, $1.75)**
Now a spectacular motion picture. **The Towering Inferno!** A
bomb explodes! Fire roars upwards in New York's newest sky-
scraper trapping world-renowned dignitaries. "The suspense is
kept very taut."—**New York Magazine**

THE OTHER SIDE OF THE MOUNTAIN   **(84-143, $1.75)**
by E. G. Valens
The story of skiing star Jill Kinmont who had to struggle back up
from total helplessness to a useful role in life. Now a Universal
film.

ROLLER BALL MURDER by William Harrison   **(76-839, $1.25)**
Thirteen short stories—intellectual shockers, jigsaw puzzles,
fables—about real people. The title story is now a major motion
picture, **ROLLERBALL,** starring James Caan.

CLASS OF '44 by Madeline Shaner   **(88-028, $1.50)**
The continuing adventures of the "Summer of '42" trio, Hermie,
Oscie and Benjie. Growing up in the forties . . . at its most
bittersweet and funny.

NIGHTMOVES by Alan Sharp   **(76-626, $1.25)**
Detective Harry Moseby knew he was crazy sticking to his business, yet he had this almost psychopathic need to follow a
problem to its end, to solve the unsolvable. Now a powerful
and provocative Warner Bros. film starring Gene Hackman.

SEE THE FILM
READ THE BOOK